A BREED APART

"I cannot get the image of you and David McCanles out of my mind," Hickok said. "Engraved in my memory, it has become a familiar and hated thing."

"Poor Jim," Sarah said, stroking his long hair. "There is no need for you to be jealous."

Hickok pulled away from her. "I cannot stand the thought of you being with me tonight and McCanles tomorrow," he said. "If you could disentangle yourself, things would be easier."

"Things would be a great deal harder," Sarah said. "David is a rough man, and he would exact a rough price if he believed there was no longer a place in my heart for him. And after he was finished beating me like an old rug, he would come for you, and you are not yet ready."

"I can stand a beating."

"Fair Jim," she said. "You misunderstand. David McCanles would not beat you—he would kill you."

A BREED APART

A Novel of Wild Bill Hickok

Max McCoy

A SIGNET BOOK

SIGNET
Published by New American Library, a division of
Penguin Group (USA) Inc., 375 Hudson Street,
New York, New York 10014, USA
Penguin Group (Canada), 90 Eglinton Avenue East, Suite 700, Toronto,
Ontario M4P 2Y3, Canada (a division of Pearson Penguin Canada Inc.)
Penguin Books Ltd., 80 Strand, London WC2R 0RL, England
Penguin Ireland, 25 St. Stephen's Green, Dublin 2,
Ireland (a division of Penguin Books Ltd.)
Penguin Group (Australia), 250 Camberwell Road, Camberwell, Victoria 3124,
Australia (a division of Pearson Australia Group Pty. Ltd.)
Penguin Books India Pvt. Ltd., 11 Community Centre, Panchsheel Park,
New Delhi - 110 017, India
Penguin Group (NZ), cnr Airborne and Rosedale Roads, Albany,
Auckland 1310, New Zealand (a division of Pearson New Zealand Ltd.)
Penguin Books (South Africa) (Pty.) Ltd., 24 Sturdee Avenue,
Rosebank, Johannesburg 2196, South Africa

Penguin Books Ltd., Registered Offices:
80 Strand, London WC2R 0RL, England

First published by Signet, an imprint of New American Library,
a division of Penguin Group (USA) Inc.

First Printing, November 2006
10   9   8   7   6   5   4   3   2   1

You say when I was murdered it was fulfilling a prophecy that all men of my kind should die with their boots on. Now I would like to know the man that prophesies how men shall die, or classes of men, so that the public may know who is right and who is wrong. I never have insulted man or woman in my life but if you knew what a wholesome regard I have for damn liars they would be liable to keep out of my way.

—James Butler Hickok, in an 1873 letter to a
    Missouri newspaper that erroneously reported
    his death by ambush

Prologue

Cheyenne
July 4, 1876

The sun was dying as the man in the black
frock coat paused in the lake of mud in the center
of camp and produced the stub of a cigar from the
left pocket of his brocaded vest. He put the cigar
in the corner of his mouth and then searched his
clothing for a match, his slender hands brushing
all of the familiar and deadly and sometimes mun-
dane things that had come to symbolize his life:
the bone-handled revolvers tucked into the red
sash, butts forward, the derringer in the right
pocket of the vest, the pint bottle of whiskey in
the inside pocket of the frock, a sheaf of letters
waiting to be posted to his wife, the scratched
and tarnished watch that hung from a silver

chain. He finally found a trio of matches in the pocket of his salt-and-pepper trousers.

He struck one match with a thumbnail but it flared and then died in the wind that blew with maddening constancy here on the northern plains. The man cussed gently and thumbed another to life, and this time the wind dwindled to a whisper and allowed him to light the cigar. Now the sounds of the camp came sharp and loud, the creaking of the wagons as the teamsters put them in file for the morning's loading, the ringing of the bell and hissing of steam as the locomotive pulled into the Union Pacific depot, the easy banter of soldiers as they lazed outside the barracks.

The man planted his boots in the mud and drew the bitter smoke into his lungs. He removed his tinted glasses and nudged the black large-brimmed hat onto the crown of his head. He peered intently to the west, where the sun was a dull red circle on the horizon. How beautiful the sun was when it was rising and setting, he thought, and so cruel when in the middle of the sky that he never dared look toward it. But now, in the twilight, he could watch with unshielded eyes at the passing of the day and give himself over to the melancholy that had dogged him since that day so long ago in Springfield. He removed the watch and cradled it in his palm as he depressed the latch and carefully allowed the cover to fold out against his fingertips. He did not care about the time. That it was late he already knew. But he read, perhaps for the thousandth time, the inscription inside.

He closed the watch and continued walking.

He mounted the wooden steps leading to the quarters of the post physician and rapped smartly on the wooden door. In the next instant, a gust of wind came from the north and blew wide the door. From inside, he could hear papers scattering like leaves.

"Damn you," a voice called. "Get in or get out, but don't just stand there. That wind will blow us all the way to Kansas."

"Damned for certain," the man said as he ducked beneath the frame and latched the door behind him. "But I doubt anything can induce me to go back to that dry, godforsaken land where the only thing the people lack more sorely than imagination is spirits."

The doctor was a fat man taking notes at a portable secretary. His legs jutted out at such an angle that it seemed he was squatting rather than sitting in the straight-backed wooden chair, and his ink-stained hand engulfed the pen.

"You're Hickok."

"I know who I am," Hickok said, removing his hat. "Not meaning to be rude, but strangers are fond of repeating the name, and I tired of it long ago."

"My apologies," the doctor said, putting down his pen and capping the well. He rose to his feet with a bit of struggle. "Let us formally introduce ourselves, then."

"James Butler Hickok."

"Mr. Frederick Carlyle, at your service."

"You're not a doctor?"

"I am a fellow of the Royal Academy of Surgeons, London."

"What in hell are you doing in Cheyenne?"

"I might well ask you the same, for I understand that the constable has sworn a warrant against you for vagrancy and that you must quit Cheyenne or face the consequences."

"I will leave when I am ready and not before," Hickok said.

"Indeed," Carlyle said, noting the revolvers tucked into Hickok's red sash. "I assume that you have come not for a social call, but are in need of my services. What is the nature of your malady?"

"Opinions differ," Hickok said.

"I understand," Carlyle said. "Allow me to examine you before you offer the opinions of the others. I have found that most of my brethren here on the plains effect more harm than good."

"We are of one mind on that account," Hickok said.

"Where is the problem?"

"My eyes."

Carlyle moved the chair to the center of the floor.

"Sit, please," he said. "Do you suffer from pain?"

"No."

"The difficulty is with your vision?"

"Yes."

"A decrease in acuity?"

"Yes."

Carlyle leaned down and peered briefly into Hickok's eyes, then stood.

"When were you first aware of it?"

"When I killed my best friend during a gunfight in Abilene five years ago. He was coming to my aid after I had killed a man who had fired two shots at me and missed."

"He was coming from the side?"

"From my right side. There was a crowd of Texans who had watched the unpleasantness, and I believed that Mike was among those meaning to do me harm."

Carlyle darkened the room by unrolling the canvas over each of the windows. "Have your eyes suffered any injury?"

"I was on the stage playacting with Cody in New York when my eyes were pierced by the spot thrown by a galvanic arc light. I suspect that the operator of the device introduced, out of spite, some filter or chemical to purposely blind me."

Carlyle lit a candle and placed himself behind Hickok.

"Tell me when you see the flame."

Hickok looked over his right shoulder.

"No, I want you to look straight ahead. Don't

move your head, and do not try to judge from the shadow cast on the wall. I want you to tell me only when you see the flame."

Carlyle advanced the candle slowly to Hickok's left. He paused a moment when the flame was even with Hickok's ear, then moved it a little farther forward and paused again.

Hickok was silent.

"How well do you see at night?"

"Not worth a damn."

"And the dark glasses I saw hanging from your coat pocket. You wear them to protect your eyes from the sunlight?"

"Yes."

"Do you frequent the Cyprian sisterhood?"

"I beg your pardon?"

"Whores, sir. Do you consort with whores?"

"It is one of my weaknesses."

"And in your sport, have you been infected by syphilis?"

"No."

"The clap, then? Have you ever received a dose and then, after touching the discharge from your member, rubbed your eyes . . . or had some remarkably intimate contact of the face with the woman's virtue that dispensed it?"

"I rarely suffer this kind of insult."

"I make no judgments; I am simply seeking information."

"I have had the clap, but engaged in none of the peculiar complications you speak of."

Carlyle pushed the flame to an angle in advance of forty-five degrees from Hickok's center of vision.

"I see it," Hickok said.

Carlyle repeated the experiment on Hickok's right side, with the same results.

He blew out the candle and unblocked the windows.

"Well?" Hickok said.

"We're not done," Carlyle said. "I want you to close your eyes, and I am going to touch them gently with my thumbs. I promise you that it might seem a bit unnatural, but it will cause you no discomfort."

"I have let no man have such an advantage."

"Do you wish my opinion or no?"

Hickok closed his eyes.

Carlyle put his hands on each side of Hickok's head and touched the balls of his thumbs to his eyelids. He pressed gently while making a slight rocking motion.

"Open your eyes."

"Have you an opinion?"

"I do," Carlyle said, and he brought up another chair so that he could speak to Hickok as a friend might. "What do people call you, sir? Do they address you as Bill or James or—"

"Jim," Hickok said.

"May I do the same?"

"You may."

"Jim, you must listen to me as if I am the voice of God, because I offer not opinion but fact. You are going blind. Your eyes are as hard as marbles, while normal eyes feel something like a hard-boiled egg."

"Marbles?"

"You have a disease that causes an unnaturally high internal pressure that distorts the eyeballs and destroys your peripheral vision. Your affliction was not caused by consorting with whores, or anything that was put into the arc lights, or by any fault of your own."

"Then how did I contract it?"

"It is congenital, perhaps," Carlyle said. "You have undoubtedly suffered for years, but the mind compensates to trick one into believing that one's field of vision remains unchanged, until something undeniable happens. Such as the killing of a true friend."

Hickok was silent.

"I don't understand how, if my eyes are so afflicted, my aim has not diminished," he said after a moment. "I can still place a ball in the center of a stamp at a hundred paces."

"That is because you retain your center of vision," Carlyle said. "As long as you can sight on something directly in front of you, in good light, there is no problem. But have you noticed that you have become increasingly suspicious of anyone behind or to the side of you, that you increasingly rely on sound to judge the approach of a potential threat?"

"I never sit with my back to the door," Hickok said. "At night, I place newspapers on the floor of my hotel room so I can hear the approach of the uninvited."

Carlyle nodded.

"You will retain your center of vision for some time, but the disease will progress until your view of the world becomes a pinhole—and finally, irrevocably, is extinguished altogether."

"How long do I have?"

"Years, perhaps," Carlyle said. "But the disease is already advanced. There is no cure, but I can recommend two things that might slow the process."

"Being?"

"The first is the alkaloid from the Calabar bean, called the doomsday plant in west Africa because it is lethal when ingested. But its extract, administered in the form of drops, is helpful in reducing the internal pressure. I have none of it here, but I can send for it. It will take some weeks."

"And the other?"

"The other I have. It is a tincture of cannabis."

"More drops?"

"No, you drink it," Carlyle said. He went to a shelf and rummaged through a number of bottles before he found the one he sought. "It also serves to relieve the pressure, and is derived from the ganja commonly used for recreation by those on the Indian subcontinent—and by some members of the English nobility. It is related to the hemp that is grown here to make rope."

"Will it make me forget?" Hickok asked.

The last thing Hickok saw was the hand he had been dealt.

He had been losing heavily all afternoon to Bill Massie, who had learned to play poker while piloting a riverboat before the war. Yesterday Hickok had taken Massie for a few dollars, but now his luck had turned and he had lost all of his pocket money to the man. A few minutes before he had taken fifteen dollars' credit in the form of house checks to continue playing.

The other men at the table were Charlie Rich, a malcontent whom Hickok had seen attempt to overturn a card table in Cheyenne when the cards ran against him, and Carl Mann, part owner of the

Number Ten Saloon where they played. They were all sitting on stools, and Rich's seat was against the wall. It was Hickok's accustomed seat, but this afternoon Rich had refused to give it up. Hickok had asked again, but Rich had teased him about his eccentricity, and Hickok had shrugged it off and remained with his back to the bar.

As Massie dealt the cards, Hickok removed his pocket watch and checked the time. It was four o'clock. They had been playing since noon. If he lost that last fifteen dollars in chips, Hickok vowed, he would quit the game and return to his friend Colorado Charley Utter's camp, where he would console himself with whiskey and then perhaps crawl between Utter's fastidiously clean sheets to sleep it off. Charley would abuse him for it, but a few moments' rest in a clean bed would be reward enough to risk Charley's short-lived wrath. It would also provide him a place to hide from the unwanted attention of Martha Jane Cannary, an unnatural creature who swore and drank like a man but had been hanging around him like a sick puppy since his arrival three weeks before in Deadwood. Hickok mistrusted women and wanted none of their company, and avoided even the whores at the notorious Gem Saloon. He felt sorry for the girls there, because the unsavory proprietor, Al Swearingen, had kidnapped many of the women and kept them under the threat of death at the hands of his thug, Johnny Burns.

Before carefully closing the lid on the watch, he

glanced at the inscription for the last time: *Mark well the hours until we meet again, my dashing Bill, for life is short and death favors all.* Then he studied the face of the Waltham repeater to determine whether the minute hand was moving. The cannabis tincture he took several times a day for his eyes gave him a not altogether unpleasant sleepy feeling and made time seem unreal, as if each moment hung in the air far too long before reluctantly fading into the next. Hickok brought the watch to his right ear, to hear the sound of the movement. He was also suddenly aware of the sound of his own pulse throbbing in his head, in unison with the ticking of the watch.

Reassured, he placed the open watch on the card table.

"What's the matter, Bill?" Rich asked. "You late for something?"

Hickok smiled without humor.

"A professional knows when to quit," Massie said easily. "Perhaps you should pack it in today, Bill, because it is a hard thing to come back from the kind of losing streak you've had this afternoon. Perhaps tomorrow will be kinder."

"Good advice," Bill allowed, "but I've beaten tougher odds, Captain. I reckon I'll stay here long enough to either humble you pirates or show you how a gentleman loses."

"That's the spirit," Massie said.

But Rich frowned.

"Let me see that," he said, then abruptly leaned over the table and reached for the watch. Hickok caught his wrist and squeezed hard enough to make Rich wince.

"I'd prefer that you didn't," Hickok said, and he was aware that his typically slow speech seemed to be coming even slower. Then he relaxed his grip.

"Hellfire, Bill," Rich said, withdrawing his smarting hand to his lap. "I just thought maybe you wanted to put up the watch to remain in the game."

"Nobody touches that watch but me," Hickok said.

"Dammit, Rich, but you are a first-rate cretin," Massie said casually as he expertly shuffled the cards. "Don't you know the story behind that regulator? Our friend Hickok once killed a man over it."

"That story true?" Rich asked.

"Who the hell knows what the truth is anymore?" Hickok said. "More lies have been told about me than about Jesus Christ. Some of them I even made up myself, to amuse the sorry scribblers who supply trash for the newspapers and the weekly magazines. But yes, the story about the watch is true. But shut up about it, because I just want to play poker."

"Hell, I didn't mean anything," Rich said. "I

just asked a question, is all. You don't have to get combative."

Hickok blinked and fixed his dilated pupils on Rich.

"Combative?" Hickok asked slowly.

"Your tone," Rich said. "You don't have to talk to me like I'm something that you wiped from the heel of your boot."

Hickok shifted slightly, adjusting his six-foot frame on the hard wooden stool. His face was relaxed, but he grasped the lapels of his Prince Albert frock, perilously close to the pair of converted Colt Navies he wore butt forward in his red sash.

"Come now," Mann said, alarmed at the tone the conversation had taken. "We run a friendly game, and there is no call for taking offense where none was meant. Allow Mr. Hickok to play in peace, and stop bickering."

"Of course," Rich said quickly. "No harm meant; I was just curious."

"I've had my fill of the curious," Hickok said.

"Apologies," Rich said. "Let me buy you a drink."

Hickok nodded, and the tension eased. Sam Young, who had been listening intently from behind the bar, brought a bottle of whiskey and filled Hickok's empty shot glass.

Hickok picked up the glass and toasted the table.

"Salud, amor, y pesetas."

He drained the glass, then rapped it on the table.

"Love and money, indeed," Massie said, then drained his own glass. "Now, let's play some cards."

Then a disheveled young man whom Hickok had cleaned out during yesterday afternoon's card game shambled in the front door of the Number Ten. His name was Jack McCall, although for some unknown reason he called himself Bill Sutherland, and Hickok had taken pity on the wretched figure with the mangled upper lip from an old wound and had given him four bits with which to buy supper.

Hickok did not see McCall take a place at the bar behind him, even though he had a view of the front door, because the light hurt his eyes. But he knew who it was because of McCall's distinctive lisp when he exchanged a few words with Sam Young. Not long after, he heard McCall shuffle toward the back door.

Hickok waited until Massie had dealt all five cards before picking them up. As he fanned them out, his heart sank. It was trash—not even a pair, and the highest card was a seven. Folklore would later have it that Hickok's last hand was a good one, a pair of aces and eights, in clubs and spades, and the jack of diamonds (or, alternately, the queen), but legend seldom equals the truth.

"You old duffer," Hickok told Massie with good nature. "You have broke me on this hand."

Then Jack McCall, who had paused at the back door, returned to stand quietly behind Hickok, a Sharps revolver in his hand. The percussion Sharps was an ugly weapon, poorly balanced and crudely made, and this one was mottled with rust and black powder stains. McCall had loaded it carelessly, having failed to properly clear the nipples before capping it. But when he pulled the trigger the hammer was over the one chamber that was sound enough to ignite, and the barrel spewed fire and smoke.

The ball entered the back of Hickok's head, passed through his brain, and shattered his upper and lower jaw, scattering teeth and blood and globs of pinkish gray matter on the card table. It continued on and lodged in the right wrist of Captain Massie, breaking the bone. Massie jumped up, thinking a pistol had accidentally discharged.

Hickok's head had pitched forward, blood dripping from his mouth, but his torso remained upright for what seemed like a very long moment. He no longer saw nor felt, but as the roar of the gunshot faded and his consciousness slid away, he heard singing—dozens of voices in perfect harmony, and above them all was the voice of an angel.

They sang of death.

Then Hickok fell backward from the stool and hit the plank floor. His black Prince Albert frock coat flew open, revealing the bone-handled converted Colt Navies still in their holsters, butt forward.

"Take that, damn you!" McCall screamed. Then he whirled, raking the muzzle of the smoking revolver around the bar. "Come on, ye sons of bitches!"

The dozen or so patrons inside the bar rushed toward the front door, with the exception of Carl Mann. He stood, cards still in his hand.

McCall pointed the revolver at Mann and pulled the trigger, and although the cap popped, the gun failed to fire. Cursing, McCall turned and impotently snapped the gun at the retreating Sam Young.

Then he dropped the revolver and ran out the back door.

Later, in the pocket of Hickok's coat, was found a letter to his wife, Agnes Lake, a former circus performer whom he had married in Cheyenne a few months earlier.

Agnes, darling, Hickok wrote, *if such should be that we never meet again, while firing my last shot, I will gently breathe the name of my wife—Agnes—and with wishes even for my enemies I will make the plunge and try to swim to the other shore.*

Hickok was thirty-nine years old.

One

The twenty-four-year-old stranger who appeared at the Rock Creek station in Nebraska Territory in the spring of 1861 walked with a limp, and his right arm was in a sling. The stranger talked little and kept to himself and did light chores around the east station with resignation, but never complained. In the evening he walked the banks of the creek as far as the abandoned mill a mile upstream and there took a spot high on the rocks overlooking the pond to spend the twilight in solitary contemplation.

He saw her one evening when the sky had turned yellow with a coming storm and she was lingering in the shadows of one of the arched stone doorways of the mill foundation. He had seen her a few times before, either at the east station or in the yard of the home nearby, tending the small garden. From the remarks of the station hands he knew her name was Sarah and that she had come from Carolina with the station owner, a hard man named McCanles who lived in the west station, on the other side of the creek, with his newly arrived family.

But this was the first time the stranger had seen her in an unguarded moment, and he was moved by the way she folded her arms and leaned against the stone of the doorway and looked longingly down the path that led to the mill. She was wearing a thin cotton dress, and as the temperature dropped and the sun went behind the trees to the east, she shivered.

Her face was hidden by her long, dark hair.

He almost called out to her, as much to relieve his own loneliness as hers, but thought better of it. Though young, he knew enough to recognize a woman who was waiting on someone, and any intrusion would certainly be unwelcome. So he contented himself to remain on his rocky perch, where his silhouette blended with the tree line behind. He settled in, drawing his knees up to his chin, and became as still as if stalking a frightened deer.

As the shadows grew longer he heard careless footsteps on the path below, and soon the lumbering figure of the station owner, Dave McCanles, came into view. The woman's face did not brighten when she saw him.

She waited in the doorway and allowed him to come to her.

"I thought you had forgotten," she said, her soft Southern voice carrying in the stillness.

"Business," McCanles said.

"Family business?" Sarah asked, her arms still folded.

McCanles grunted his displeasure.

"Your wife," Sarah said. "Why did you send for her?"

"Because she is my wife," McCanles said. "The mother of my children. It is the way of things."

"She cannot be charmed with the arrangement."

"No," McCanles allowed. "She is not charmed."

The stranger was ashamed to be spying on them, but could not easily leave his spot without being noticed.

"And I?" Sarah said. "Do you not ponder what I am charmed by? Do you no longer care for my happiness, as you pledged you did so long ago and so far away? Do you not remember the tender words you spoke when you took me from my father's home to this place that you promised would be paradise, but has for me instead become purgatory? Do you not care for the sin you have committed?"

"I have committed no sin," McCanles said. He was a big man, tall and heavily muscled, and he had an easy way with both men and women. "The Bible says that adultery is committed only

with a married woman. You belong to no man, so
I commit no sin."

"And what of me, David?" she asked. "Am I
without sin as well?"

He reached for her suddenly, grasping her by
the wrist. She attempted to pull away, back into
the shadows of the mill, but he jerked her to him as
one might a child.

"You are full of sin," he said.

He swept her into his arms and kissed her hard
on the mouth while she attempted to push away.
When they parted, she slapped him across the
face. McCanles laughed, then backhanded her
hard enough to send her sprawling on the ground.
She lay in the dirt at his feet, her eyes blazing, a
trickle of blood running from the corner of her
mouth.

"Damn you," she said, tears brimming.

The stranger on the rock shifted, his good hand
reaching for the butt of the revolver at his belt. He
released his grip on the gun when he saw the
woman kiss McCanles with passion, the blood
smearing both of their faces. When she glanced up,
the stranger could have sworn that she was looking beyond McCanles's shoulder at him.

"Is that what you wanted?" Sarah asked Mc-
Canles, her chest heaving. "To taste my blood? Is it
salty or sweet, David? When you lay with your
wife, does she offer her blood as well? Does she
offer you anything to compare to this?"

Then Sarah slipped the straps from her shoulders and her dress fell to the ground. She wore nothing beneath, and her body shone like a ghost in the failing light. Her breasts were full and her stomach was gently rounded, and McCanles picked her up and pressed her roughly against the stone of the doorway.

"Does she love you as I love you?" Sarah asked. "Has she sacrificed as I have sacrificed? Has she ever given you the pleasure that I have given so freely?"

McCanles fumbled with his buckle, removed his belt with the heavy revolver, and dropped it on the ground. Then he lowered his trousers. As he entered her with force, she cried out and buried her head against his neck. Then she brought up her knees and folded her ankles around his back so that she could take him more deeply.

The stranger knew he should look away, but could not.

The storm came after McCanles left.

Sarah huddled in the doorway of the mill while the stranger remained impotently on the rock, water pouring from the brim of his cheap slouch hat.

"You, there," Sarah called suddenly. "Come down from that damned rock and talk to me."

He hesitated.

"Don't be bashful," she urged. "I know you're there. You're always there this time of evening.

Don't be ashamed of what you saw, for I have no shame."

"Then I am sorry for you," he said.

The woman laughed. It was a harsh sound and carried no trace of mirth.

"I am indeed a sorry sight," she said. "Are you to leave me as well?"

He unlimbered his frame, which had always seemed too long and lean to be of much use, and used his one good hand to ease himself over the rock. As his boots touched the ground, lightning ripped through the sky and split the top of a cottonwood near the mill, showering the ground with embers, and he could feel the rumble of the blast in the balls of his feet.

"You'd best hurry," she called. "Or would being struck dead by lightning please you more than passing a few moments with me?"

He found the path and walked with a measured stride. Another blast of thunder engulfed him, and although he felt the urge to run twitching in his legs and feet, he checked himself.

"Doesn't anything scare you?" she asked as he drew near.

"You do."

She smiled.

He slipped his injured arm from the sling and, with some difficulty, removed his rough coat and, with one hand, draped it around her shoulders. Before he tucked his right arm back into the cloth cradle, she glimpsed the ugly wound just above the wrist.

"What's your name?"

"Hickok."

"Your Christian name."

"James."

"Well, Jim," she said. "You certainly are an enigma here. Wish I could say the same for myself. You do know what the word means, enigma?"

"You mistake me for a moron," he said. "I am quiet, but not unlettered. I come from a good family in Illinois that would be shamed to know that I hid skulking in the shadows during your encounter. I apologize that I was witness to a private moment. In truth I would have slipped away but for fear of drawing attention to myself and causing you embarrassment."

"I am not embarrassed, Jim," she said, her green eyes meeting his. "I have known for some time about your rock, where you ponder the unfathomable world. Secretly, I had hoped you might be here this very evening."

"Why?"

"Why not?" she asked. "The truth is liberating, don't you think? While the McCanles wife is secure in her trappings of respectability, what is the harm in sharing the truth with a compassionate stranger who watches the world but declines to participate? At least now there is no pretense between us. This evening I have heard you speak more words than in all of your weeks at the station, and I am pleased to find your speech so far from the crudeness that passes for conversation among the lost souls who find themselves in this godforsaken place."

"I beg your pardon," he said. "I am uncomfortable with the events of the previous instant. Perhaps I should take my leave, or better yet see you safely to your home. In either case, I will embrace the pretense that I have seen nothing that might diminish your character in the eyes of others. As Christ said, 'Let he who is without sin cast the first stone.' "

"Familiar with Scripture as well," Sarah said. "My Jim, how you do amaze. Do you mean to tell me that here on the frontier you have never witnessed sport?"

"Only with women who are professionally inclined," he said. "And that I do not take you for."

"All women are professionally inclined. It is simply a matter of degree. What else does a woman have to trade for security in this world?"

"My mother would be an exception."

"Ah, that is a comforting thought," she said. "Untrue, but comforting. Oh, Jim, don't look so hurt. Do you think that you came into this world as Christ himself did? And how better for your mother to secure her affections in your father's eyes?"

"Speak no more of my family."

"Agreed," she said. "But before you escort me back to my prison at Rock Creek station, perhaps we should wait until the storm is spent, lest we find ourselves split as surely as that cottonwood."

He nodded.

"Besides," she continued, "I feel more at home here. My father owned a mill before McCanles carried me away, and I draw comfort here."

He could not imagine anyone drawing comfort from the structure. The roof was open to the sky, as the mill had been abandoned after the rafters were up but before the planks and shingles were laid, and the rain was pouring in. The only shelter was beneath the doorway in the thick limestone foundation.

"Why do you suppose this was never finished?" he asked.

"There was every intention, I suppose," she said. "There were thousands of immigrants on the Oregon Trail last year, but now that war has come the number has dwindled to a handful. Let us sit here for a while, and you can tell me the story of your broken wing."

She slid to the ground, her back against the stone, and he did so on the opposite side of the doorway.

"It is a trifle," he said.

"Assuredly not," she said. "You have lost the use of your right hand, and that puts a man at a disadvantage so far from civilization. How badly is the arm broken?"

"Badly enough," he said.

She smiled.

Hickok looked into her green eyes.

"You keep your secrets well," she said. "That is good. But tell me true, how well can you use this?"

Her hand touched the butt of the revolver. It was a Colt Navy, and he wore it tucked into the right side of his broad leather belt, butt forward, so that his left hand might easily grasp it. It was the only possession he had of any value, and he was fanatical in his care of it.

He grasped her wrist with his free hand.

"Are you to handle me as McCanles did?"

"No," he said, suddenly embarrassed.

"Are you afraid I might take the advantage?"

"You had that when you first spoke," he said. "But no, I do not fear that you will shoot me."

"Then allow me a glance," she said, and with her right hand deftly slipped the revolver out of its holster. The gun glistened with oil, and the brass strap shone brightly between the walnut grips.

"It is chilly to the touch," she said.

She ran her fingers over the cylinder, feeling the engraved naval battle that twisted around it, then traced the top of the octagonal barrel down to the beaded front sight. Suddenly she hooked her right thumb over the hammer and attempted to cock the gun, but did not have the strength. Her hand quivered and the hammer slipped from beneath the ball of her thumb and snapped back onto the nipple.

The muzzle was inches from Hickok's gut.

She let out a cry of surprise.

He took the gun from her.

"Only a fool keeps the hammer over a hot chamber," he said as he awkwardly returned the gun to the holster. "The other five are quite ready to fire. I would appreciate your not touching the piece again."

"I know little about guns."

"That much is evident."

"But I know enough to recognize an expensive weapon when I see it," she said. "That is not the sort of item one would expect to find on a crippled station hand, is it? You are too tall to be an Express rider. From the look of your buckskins, I would take you for a scout, fallen on hard times. Is that it?"

"It might be."

"Tell me true, Jim. How is your quickness and your aim?"

"Bragging does not become me," he said.

"Do you know what Dave calls you? Duck Bill."

"I was called Dutch Bill in Kansas."

"Why?"

"Because every other fool on the frontier is named James, and you can't keep track of all the

Jims without tripping. But McCanles is having some fun at my expense."

"Ah, you're sensitive about your looks. Don't worry, Jim; I find your features to be rather dashing. Your nose is Romanesque and your eyes are as blue as the evening sky but as cold as steel. And your hands . . . they are as delicate as a girl's."

She now had taken his left hand and turned the palm up. She traced his slender fingers with her other hand, and as she did she made a soft sound in her throat.

"Can you shoot with this hand?"

"I favor the other," he said, taking back his hand.

From his pocket he brought a faded kerchief and held it awkwardly to her.

"Your mouth," he said. "Don't worry; it's clean."

"It will stain," she said.

"Please," he said.

She dabbed the corner of her mouth.

"How old are you?"

"How old do you think I am?"

"I don't know," Hickok said. "Twenty-eight, maybe."

"Then I am," she said, and smiled. Then she placed her palm on his buckskin shirt, over his heart. "There is trouble coming, my fair Jim. McCanles is anxious for his money from the Overland Company so that he can take his family south. You are at risk because you are in the company's service. McCanles is not a gentleman."

"Neither am I."

"Don't bluff me, Jim," she said. "Your cards are painfully upon the table. Let's see . . . you had dreams of the West and they were dashed somehow. A woman, perhaps, or cards. It doesn't matter how. But you are not a man who has learned to take defeat in stride. You've a lesson to learn here, should you stay, and if you fail you risk not worldly things, but your very life."

"I'm staying."

"No hesitation, then," she said. "You must promise me one thing: You must not fall in love with me. I will help you in every way a woman can help a man. I can relieve the ache in your soul, Jim. But when the trouble is over, I will be gone. Do you understand?"

"No," he said.

"You will," she said. "Some night you will find me on your rock at sunset, if you wish. Don't answer now. I can find my way home, and I will return what passes for your coat later. Go and practice drawing that piece with your left hand so that you may be sure of yourself when the time comes."

She kissed him and then ran into the rain, leaving him with the taste of blood on his lips.

Two

At dawn Hickok stood on the bank of the creek. His habit each morning was to empty his pistol and then carefully reload, because he had witnessed too many weapons, either from drawing moisture or being carelessly cleaned or loaded in the first place, misfire when they were needed most. Since losing the use of his right hand, however, he had approached this ritual casually, discharging the Navy into the creek as quickly as he could cock and fire.

But this morning he found a rotting log and, with his heel, kicked a chunk away. Then he pitched the chunk upstream. As it floated by, not fifteen yards away, he deliberately drew and cocked his revolver. With his right eye, he sighted down the barrel, aligning the notches in the rear of the hammer with the bead sight, and squeezed the trigger with his left forefinger.

The revolver barked and the bullet zipped into the water a foot above the mark. As the wood floated away, he cocked and fired twice quickly, but the results were even more disappointing.

As the last gunshot echoed along the creek, a pair of crows mocked him from the opposite bank.

"You say that now," Hickok said.

He replaced the gun in the holster and kicked another chunk from the log. This time he gave it a good throw, nearly pitching it to the opposite bank.

He drew the gun and sighted as before, but then paused. There was an unnatural tension in his neck. He blinked, then turned his head slightly to the right, and the tension eased. He allowed his left eye to follow the barrel to the target, and when he fired, the round dimpled the water a few inches below the wood. He cocked and fired again, and this round took a notch from the top of the wood.

He replaced the gun in the holster.

The wood had now drifted to a bend in the creek, nearly out of sight. He drew and fired his last shot, missing by a yard.

The crows laughed raucously.

Three

Sarah had spread a blanket on the rock and was sitting with her knees drawn to one side. Hickok climbed up onto the rock and sat down beside her.

She turned to look at him, and her dark hair cascaded in front of her eyes. She brushed the hair away and smiled.

"I wasn't sure you'd come," she said.

"Neither was I," he said. He leaned back and propped himself on his good elbow.

"I was here last night," she said. "I waited until it got too dark to see. No, it's all right. It gave me time to think. I realized that I've been waiting for you all of my life."

She leaned close and kissed him slowly.

"Whatever you can imagine, I will do," she said. "Care to feel like Adam before the fall? Then I am your Eve. Long to feel like a god yourself? Then you are Zeus and I am your swan. Whatever you want me to be—"

"Please," Hickok said.

"Why does this distress you so?" Sarah asked. "A woman like me has certain advantages. I require no expenditure of effort to be won, no soft words or faithless promises."

She brushed her hair from her face.

"I can bear you no children. A happy thing, no? Sport without regret. No pitiful souls to drag into this world. So, there are no strings attached, no brats to feed, no wedding troth to dull our shame."

"You know nothing of me."

"Your discomfort," she said. "Explain it to me."

"You do enough talking for the both of us."

"Would you prefer that I be a boy for you?"

She peered intently at Hickok.

"My meaning is lost, isn't it?"

"I can scarcely forget that you are a woman," he said. "How can I? It is all I think about. The way the rain plastered your hair against you, the way you looked at me, and the things you said. The touch of your lips."

She smiled.

"And the trouble?"

"I cannot get the image of you and David McCanles out of my mind," he said. "Engraved in my memory, it has become a familiar and hated thing."

"Poor Jim," she said, stroking his long hair.

"It has fired my anger," Hickok said. "I am ashamed to admit that I am often quite lost in schoolboy fantasies of taking my revenge. At the same time, I realize no offense has been committed against me. Why do I feel this way? Simply because I am utterly and unjustifiably jealous."

"There is no need for you to be jealous," she said, and kissed him on the forehead. "Stop brooding and learn to feel. You do remember what it is like to feel?"

He pulled away from her. "No, I cannot stand the thought of you being with me tonight and McCanles tomorrow," he said. "If you could disentangle yourself, things would be easier."

"Things would be a great deal harder," Sarah said. "David is a rough man, and he would exact a rough price if he believed there was no longer a place in my heart for him. And after he was finished beating me like an old rug, he would come for you, and you are not yet ready."

"I can stand a beating."

"Fair Jim," she said. "You misunderstand. David McCanles would not beat you—he would kill you."

Four

The old man sat on a wooden crate placed in the sun on the east side of the barn. He hugged his knees while a cat with filthy white fur twisted around his ankles. Hickok brought a blanket from the barn and slung it across the man's lap.

"Cold today," Hickok said.

The cat jumped into the old man's lap.

"Didn't used to get so cold," the man said, stroking the cat. A wicked scar ran from his forehead to his left jaw, and the eye on that side of his face had turned to milk. "If it did, I didn't feel it."

"Always gets cold."

The old man laughed.

"In 'twenty-seven, up around the Clark Fork of the Missouri, I waded out every day into creeks filled with snowmelt and never thought a thing of it. I didn't have nothing but my rifle and my traps, and I damn near starved. The peculiar thing was, I was happy."

"Happy to be alive, I reckon."

"No, it wasn't like that," the old man said. "I didn't give a damn. The Blackfeet stole my horse, and they could have taken my hair anytime the notion suited them, but I didn't care. I owed nobody a thing. If I lived to rendezvous, that was gravy."

Hickok sat down on the stump used to chop kindling and took an apple from his pocket. He offered it to the old man.

"Can't eat it," he said. "Teeth are too bad."

Hickok placed the apple on the stump beside him, drew his patch knife with his good hand, and awkwardly quartered it. The apple was green and tough.

"Want a slice?"

"Nope," the old man said.

"What happened?" Hickok said.

"Time happened," the old man said. "Changes everything. After a dozen winters in the mountains I got tired of drinking and gambling away everything I made, and my bones started to ache, and I settled here with Jane's mother and tried my hand at farming. Never was worth a damn at it. By and by my woman caught a fever and died when Jane was small, and we were alone up until this Wellman fellow came."

"Wellman," Hickok said. "The station boss."

"The same," the old man said, then spit. "That

one, he has the soul of a merchant. Always bragging about how the stage company and the Pony Express would make him rich, how there would always be work, what with stations strung out every five miles all the way from St. Joe to Sacramento. Well, I guess the war has changed his mind about that."

"He seems pleasant enough."

"He is," the old man said. "That's the way of merchants, all smiles while they're thinking about your money. There's more to life than a ledger book, boy."

"Reckon so."

"Jane, now she's the one to watch," the old man said. "Takes after her mother. Both of them meaner than snakes."

"That's a tender sentiment."

"Shows what you know about women," the old man said. "They are a cold breed. There's nothing as vicious on God's earth as a woman who is trying to protect what is hers ... or trying to take something that ain't."

Hickok laughed.

"Oh, I chased my share of split tail," the old man said. "In my prime, when my rod was yet stiff, I walked fearless and empty-handed into places where I wouldn't go now with a double load of buckshot. See this scar? Got my eye gouged out in Santa Fe over a pretty little brown gal that had no discernible heart."

"Was it worth it?"

"Thought so," the old man said. "But now I know there ain't nothing pretty about the nether reaches of a woman. Damned if I know why we fight so hard to get a glimpse of it. But there's a reason that slimy thing is tucked down there near where they shit. Know what I'm saying, boy?"

"Can't say that I do."

"I'm talking about that viper that lives in the far house," the old man said. "The Shull woman. She has the stench of death about her."

"She doesn't smell nearly as bad as that cat of yours."

"Ain't nothing wrong with President Jefferson. Is there, Tom?" the old man said. "He thinks no less of me for my opinions, or that my days are reduced to waiting on the next coach in hopes that it will bring a tin of oysters. But the coaches have gotten as scarce as hen's teeth these days."

"That they have."

"What in hell happened to your arm?"

"Bear," Hickok said.

"Bears don't leave clean breaks."

"The kind I tangled with does."

The old man laughed.

"Thought so," he said. "You can tell me the story sometime over a glass of whiskey. Say, you wouldn't happen to have any whiskey, would you?"

"Not a drop," Hickok said. "You drank the last of it, remember?"

The old man grunted.

"Just as well," he said. "When I drink, that Shull woman begins to look mighty good. Women and whiskey make fools of us all, boy, and there ain't no sadder fool than an old fool."

"I don't think you're a fool," Hickok said.

"I understand now why Tom likes you."

"Well, you can thank the president for me," Hickok said, "but you can tell him that I still find his odor as offensive as that of a common skunk. He has ruined my appetite."

Hickok tossed the remains of the apple into the yard.

The cat stood, arched its back, and stared down the road. Then it jumped from the old man's lap and flew off into the barn.

"Hope it wasn't something I said."

"It's that damned McCanles and the two Jims," the old man said. "Tom can't stand them, and neither can I."

A dog raced into the stock pen ahead of the horsemen. It sniffed at the ground around Hickok's feet, and then its nose found his hand. Hickok idly scratched the dog's head while McCanles and his hired men, James Woods and James Gordon, rode into the stock pen.

Woods was a small man who seemed perpetually dirty and always seemed to be sneering.

Gordon was corpulent and appeared slightly cross-eyed.

McCanles swung down from the saddle and threw his reins to Woods. He took off his slouch hat with the turkey feather in the band and tossed it to Hickok, who caught it by the brim with his left hand.

"Don't let that hat touch the ground," McCanles said. He walked across the yard, swept off the lid of the rain barrel, and plunged both hands into the water. He washed his face, letting the water drip down his beard and chin and then back into the barrel.

Then McCanles stood, put his hands behind his back, and stretched.

"Homer, where is that idiot son-in-law of yours?"

"Don't know," the old man said.

"Well, I am due my payment from the Express company," McCanles said as he walked lazily over to the crate where the old man sat. "I am a patient man, but my patience does have limits. You, Duck Bill. You receive any word about my payment?"

Hickok ignored him.

"Are you deaf or just a moron?" McCanles asked. "I asked you a question. You work for the company. Do you know anything about my money?"

Hickok examined the hat.

"I'll be shaved," McCanles said. "Am I going to have to playact the question for you?"

"I don't know anything about your money," Hickok said as he ran his thumb over the turkey feather. "And what you called me, that ain't my name. I'll thank you not to use it."

McCanles roared with laughter.

"You'll thank me in either case, I allow," he said. "And since we are finally having what may pass, by an extreme stretch of mind, for a conversation, perhaps you can clear up a little mystery that has accompanied your person since you joined us here at Rock Creek station. Who in hell busted you up so?"

"Nobody," Hickok said.

"It was an accident, then."

"It was no accident."

"What, then?" McCanles asked with exaggerated interest.

Hickok stared at him.

"It was a bear," the old man said.

Hickok shot him a wicked glance.

"A grizzly," the old man added.

"A bear?" McCanles asked, his eyes flashing. "A grizzly! We are to believe that this rawhide strip of a boy with beak attached went toe-to-toe with old Ephraim and lived to tell of it? Tell us, pilgrim, how did you hasten the demise of the great beast and effect your own escape? Did you fire a ramrod into its skull? A bowie, perhaps, driven deep into its black ursine heart? Or perhaps you just stared it to death, as you are attempting to do with me now?"

"I killed no bear," Hickok said.

"Of course you didn't," McCanles said, "for you are a great liar."

"I don't lie."

"No, you just have Homer the Hapless do your lying for you," McCanles said. "And speaking of which, Homer, you owe me for the bottle of whiskey kept in the barn that mysteriously emptied itself less than a fortnight ago. Unless, of course, the great bear slayer will account for it. Or would that be another lie, my one-armed friend?"

"I didn't drink it," Hickok said.

"Ah, and what of you, Homer?" McCanles said. "Did you drink it?"

McCanles walked toward the crate on which Homer sat.

"I don't remember," the old man said.

McCanles kicked the crate out from under him, and the man landed heavily on the ground. The crash frightened the dog, who at one jump seemed to put several yards between him and the unpleasant sound.

As the old man's face drew tight in pain, Hickok glanced over at the two Jims and saw that Gordon already had a shotgun slung over his saddle and that Woods held an old dragoon pistol in the crook of his arm.

"Does that help your memory?"

"Can't recommend it," the old man sputtered.

McCanles shook his head.

"You are one cocky sonuvabitch to be so damned old," he said. "How old are you, Homer?"

"Don't know."

"Damn, you don't know much, do you?" McCanles said, then backhanded the old man across the face. "Now, did that help your memory? Do you recall the year of your birth or my bottle of whiskey?"

Hickok's hand twitched toward his revolver, the same as his legs had wanted to run when the lightning had struck nearby. But Homer caught his glance and, while wiping blood from his mouth, shook his head.

Hickok let his hand go limp.

"We used that whiskey for the care of the stock," McCanles said. "It was rotgut, and any sorry specimen who drank it would risk blindness."

"I drank your fucking whiskey," the old man said.

"Ah, your memory returns," McCanles said.

"It does indeed," the old man said, struggling to his knees. "And I thought about you while I drank it, Dave, and I thought about you again when I pissed it out."

As McCanles moved toward him, the old man drew an old trade knife. He lunged at McCanles, who easily dodged the attack and sent the toe of his boot into his ribs. Hickok winced as he heard bones snap like dry sticks.

"Old bastard," McCanles said.

He turned toward Hickok.

"I'll have my hat now," he said.

Hickok dropped the hat on the ground.

McCanles smiled as he leaned over to pick up his hat. He brushed the dirt away, adjusted the turkey feather, then placed the hat upon his head.

"That was very stupid," McCanles said. "Why don't you go for your gun? I'd like that very much. So would my friends."

Gordon cocked both barrels of the shotgun.

"The way I see it, all of you are just squatters here until I get my money." He turned to his men. "Isn't that the way you see it, boys?"

"Damn right," Woods said. "Squatters."

Gordon scratched his beard and tried to look thoughtful. He failed, however, because of his crossed eyes.

"Looks like they ought to be paying you some kind of rent," he said. "All you have so far is promises, Dave, and promises don't spend. You'd be within your rights to run 'em off at your pleasure."

"You're right, I know," McCanles said. "But I just don't have it in me. Call me a fool, but don't ever let it be said that I lacked warmth. I will bide my time a little while longer, in the expectation that the stage company will do the right thing and fulfill its end of the deal."

"That's big of you, Dave," Woods said.

"Yes, I know," McCanles said. He turned to leave, but paused. "Oh, I almost forgot." With one motion he drew his revolver and struck Hickok across the forehead, sending him sprawling.

"Don't ever cross me again," McCanles said.

McCanles swung up into the saddle, and Woods threw him the reins. Gordon whistled for the dog.

Five

Horace Wellman carried the old man into the house, ducked beneath a patchwork quilt that divided the room, and placed him on a bed near the wall. Wellman's common-law wife, Jane, looked up from the hearth in horror.

"What happened?" she asked.

"McCanles busted him up," Hickok said, stepping into the cabin. He walked slowly, because his head ached from the blow McCanles had given him in parting. It was the first time he had been in the Wellman home, even though it was only a few dozen yards from the barn and stock pen.

"Cocksucking bastard," Jane said as she hung the coffeepot over the flames. Her skirt was bunched up over her knees, and her exposed shin was as hairy as a man's. Then she stood and walked over to the old man. She placed a hand beneath his chin and inspected his bloody face. "Where's he hurt worst?"

"It's his ribs, ma'am," Hickok said. "McCanles stove a few of them in, I think."

"How?"

"Kicked him," Hickok said.

The old man's eyes fluttered.

"Like a dog," he said. "Christ, sit me up a bit. I can't breathe."

"It's okay, Pa," Jane said, propping a pillow beneath him. Then she turned to Hickok. "Why did he kick him?"

"McCanles accused him of stealing whiskey."

"No call for a beating," Jane said, removing the old man's shirt. "Why, you wouldn't treat an animal this way."

"Dave McCanles *is* an animal," Sarah Shull said as she stepped forward and handed Jane a wet handkerchief. It was the same kerchief that Hickok had given her. The stain had not come out. "That McCanles would do just about anything as long as he had the advantage. Don't you think, Mister Hickok?"

"It appears so," Hickok said.

"Did he give you that knot on your forehead?"

"Indeed," Hickok said.

Jane had the old man's shirt unbuttoned. She placed her face on his bare chest, listening.

"His breathing don't sound right," Jane said. "Bill, get over here and give a listen."

"Ma'am, I'm afraid I know very little about diagnosing ailments."

"You know what a normal person's heart sounds like, don't you? Just get over here and give a listen."

"All right," Hickok said, then stepped forward. He knelt at the edge of the bed, then placed his cheek against the old man's chest. He tried to ignore the stench of the old man's body and concentrate instead on the sound of his breathing.

"There does appear to be some liquid kind of sound," Hickok said. "There is no froth on his lips, such as when an animal is lung-shot. But the sound is queer. I just don't know what it means."

"It ain't good," Wellman said.

"Somebody must fetch the sawbones," Jane said.

"I'll go," Hickok said.

"It's two days' ride," Wellman said.

"Are you up to it?" Sarah asked.

"Yes, I'm up to it," Hickok said. "Besides, I'm the only hand Wellman can spare. It's not like I've been able to do a helluva lot of work around the place."

The old man grasped the front of Hickok's shirt and pulled him close.

"When I die," he said, "I want you to kill that filthy sonuvabitch. Do it with my gun." The old man waved a hand toward the old half-stock plains rifle hanging from the wall over the bed.

"Promise me," the old man said with difficulty.

Hickok shook his head.

The old man coughed violently, then managed: "Promise."

"I make no such promise," Hickok said. "Besides, you'll be able to shoot him yourself, once you get back on your feet."

Six

By the time Hickok returned, the filthy white cat was sitting alone on the wooden crate on the east side of the barn, taking in the morning sun.

"I'm afraid we are too late," Hickok said, swinging down from his horse.

"How do you know?"

"The cat," Hickok said.

"Sonuvabitch," the surgeon said. "What a waste of my time."

Hickok smiled.

The surgeon was a painfully thin man in worn black clothing, and he peered at the world through a pair of thick pince-nez glasses.

"I'm sure the old man felt a bit more inconvenienced," Hickok said.

"I still get paid," the surgeon said.

"You will get it," Hickok said. "But only after I

put up the horses and we get a bite to eat from the grieving daughter. Mind your manners and act like you're sorry you arrived too late to help."

"Now, what about that arm?"

"What about it?" Hickok asked.

"It ain't healing right," the surgeon said. "At least, not judging from the angle of your hand. It may need to be reset, or . . ."

"Or what?"

"Or you might never get full use of it again."

"Don't worry about my arm," Hickok said. "Come, let's get you fed, and afterward you can pass a few hours here and catch a ride back to town on the Leavenworth and Pikes Peak Coach . . . if it runs today."

"It had better be at company expense," the surgeon said.

"Everything is," Hickok said as he loosened the cinch strap beneath his horse's belly. "Seems that's all the company has these days is expenses."

"Are you an Express rider?" the surgeon asked. "Put temporarily out of work by your injury?"

"You've not been west long, have you? No, I'm not a rider . . . too damn tall. The riders are little fellows, so as to be easy on the horses and save more weight for mail."

They met Sarah Shull outside the cabin.

"Where'd they bury him?" Hickok asked.

"On the hill overlooking the creek," Sarah said, her arms folded. "He wanted to be buried in the trees, and they promised they would, but Jane couldn't stand the thought of her father's bones being picked clean by crows."

"Coffin?"

"No, just wrapped him in a blanket," Sarah said. "Don't feel bad, Jim. You couldn't have saved him. He died the night you rode out."

Hickok was silent.

"What's for supper?" the surgeon asked.

"What is always for supper," Sarah said. "We have turtle soup, and if you don't like that, we got turtle soup. I used to like turtle soup, but it becomes a mite monotonous after a year or two. But it's cheap, and that's what counts."

"It's not bad," Hickok said.

"You've only been eating it for three weeks."

Jane appeared at the door of the cabin.

Hickok removed his hat.

"I'm sorry," he said. "Miss Shull has just confirmed the worst. Please accept my sympathy and know that while your father could neither read nor write, he and his kind left their mark on the land as few have done. He deserves our every respect."

"Thank you," Jane said.

"I heard a rumor of turtle soup?"

"You must be the sawbones."

"Yes, madam."

"Then you might as well confirm the diagnosis."

"It would be my pleasure."

"You, Hickok," Jane said. "Aren't you hungry?"

"Not at present," Hickok said. "I believe Miss Shull and I have some business to discuss. You will excuse us?"

Hickok touched Sarah's elbow as they walked down the path to the rough-hewn bridge across the creek.

"They've got venison at the west house," Sarah said.

"Indeed," Hickok said.

"This is the first damned thing Dave built here," she said as she stopped in the middle of the bridge. She leaned against the rail and watched the water flowing beneath. "When I asked what he was going to charge for a toll, he said, 'All they can stand.' At one point he was getting fifty cents a family, and they were lining up. Then things slacked off and he dropped the price to ten cents. Even at that, some of them preferred to hike upstream to where the mill is and cross at that rocky ford. Now traffic is so light he doesn't bother charging a red cent."

"Were things good then?"

"Good enough," Sarah said. "It was exciting, you know. I had never been anywhere outside of Watauga County. Dave was sheriff, and every man in the county was afraid of him, badge or no. I see now that he was just a common bully. Then he got into trouble over collecting debts that never made it to the county treasury, and then I got into trouble."

"What kind of trouble?"

"The usual kind," Sarah said. "I had his child, but the poor thing died. We buried her in the dead of night. Not long after, what with the county fixing to throw Dave in his own jail, we took off. Our goal was the Kansas goldfields. But we never made it. After meeting hundreds of the disappointed coming back down the trail, Dave decided we would settle here, and bought this little station. He dug a well and built this toll bridge. He figured if we couldn't strike it rich, he would get rich off the fools who thought they could. And it worked, for a while. Then, when it was clear the war was coming, he sent for his family. That was the end of 'good enough.' "

"He's a rebel."

"Don't tell me that surprises you."

"I've known men like him before," Hickok said. "He and the border ruffians in Kansas are cut from the same cloth. For all of their dash, they are common thieves and cutthroats."

"Dave is an uncommon cutthroat, I'd say."

"Has he been around since the old man died, either to express regret or add further insult?"

"No. I assumed he had ridden off on business. God knows he has his hand in every little thing for thirty miles around. I doubt if he even knows the old man has died. But he wouldn't care, even if he did know."

Hickok was silent.

"Here," Sarah said, offering a cigar. "I have been

saving these. The coach came along the day after you left, and I bought a handful. I was hoping we could smoke in celebration of victory over death. Sadly, it looks as if we will have to smoke to console ourselves."

"I don't smoke," Hickok said.

Sarah laughed.

"Oh, the next thing you'll tell me is that you're a Yankee," she said. She bit away the end of the cigar, stuck it in the corner of her mouth, and struck a match. After a few puffs, she offered it to Hickok.

"No," he said.

"I'll be damned."

"Twice over," Hickok said, "for I am also a Yankee. My folks had a secret room in our basement that was used as a stop on the Underground Railroad. When my father died, my uncle took over the work. So, I am not merely a Yankee, but an abolitionist."

Sarah shook her head and laughed.

"Take the cigar, Jim," she advised. "Out here, even the women smoke. Don't worry. It ain't so bad once you get used to the taste."

Hickok took the cigar and puffed.

"There you go," she said. "It'll make you sicker than a dog, but that will pass. Pretty soon you'll so look forward to that first smoke of the day that you'll be waking up early for it."

"I can't imagine," Hickok said, taking the cigar

from his mouth and looking at it with disgust. He started to pitch it into the creek, but Sarah stopped him.

"Don't waste it," she said, and drew it from his hand. She took a long drag, then let the smoke trail from her nostrils. "I hope his wife chokes on it."

"I beg your pardon?"

"The venison," Sarah said. Then she brightened. "You know, it is getting warmer. Before long it will be warm enough for me to start sleeping in the attic again. I really prefer it, since the outside ladder presents easy access without disturbing the household."

Seven

Doc Brinks took the plate of food from Jane, then reached over and tore a piece of bread from the loaf on the table. He was about to sit when Jane hooked the leg of the chair with her toe and drew it away.

"Riders eat outside."

"I am tired, sore, and starved unto death," Brinks complained. "I have put more miles beneath me in the last three weeks than most men will see in their entire life, and this is my reward?"

"I'm not cleaning up your mess," she said. "Outside. And make sure to bring the plate and the spoon back when you're done."

Brinks cursed.

"Come on," Hickok said. "I'll keep you company."

"Don't you have work to do?"

"Yes, but I'd hear the news first."

The men walked outside, and Brinks looked disapprovingly at the yard.

"It's all mud," he said.

"At least it's soft."

Brinks muttered, tested a spot with his boot, and declared it reasonably dry. He sat down crosslegged, rested the plate in his lap, and withdrew a newspaper from inside his shirt.

"Leavenworth paper," Brinks said. "Two days ago. Says Lincoln has called for a volunteer army of four hundred thousand men to fight the rebels."

Hickok took the paper and sat down next to Brinks.

"Governor Robinson has commissioned a Kansas regiment and they're mustering at Fort Leavenworth," Brinks said. "I imagine that old jayhawker Jim Lane will have a taste of the action—if there is anything to be stolen along the way."

"Lane has his own brigade," Hickok said. "What is the climate along the border?"

"Tight as a fiddle string," Brinks said. "Missouri is split right down the middle. Claiborne Jackson, the secesh governor, ordered the state militia to encamp outside of St. Louis in preparation for seizing the armory, which holds enough guns to arm every rebel this side of the Mississippi. But Nathaniel Lyon and his band of Germans arrested the militia and paraded them through the streets of St. Louis. Some of the citizens took exception. A fight broke out. The soldiers killed at least a score before they were stopped."

"What's the reaction?"

"Governor Price has come out of retirement to call for secession. The rebels have added a thirteenth star to their flag, even though they have only half the state. Steamboat traffic is shut down. Union folks that live in the thulies are packing up and heading for the nearest Yankee fort, while the secesh are spoiling for a fight."

"Any shooting yet?"

"Always shooting on the border," Brinks said through a mouthful of turtle soup. "But if you mean the kind of stand-up shooting armies do, I ain't heard of any. Springfield will be the place for action, since the rebels have already lost the big armory."

"Springfield," Hickok said.

"It is one helluva freight depot," Brinks said. "Down in the southwestern corner of the state, perched just above rebel Arkansas.

"What's the matter, Bill?"

"It'll all be over before I get out of here."

"Hell, that arm ought to be nearly healed," Brinks said.

"No, it isn't," Hickok said. "Doc, how many horses have you tended with broken legs?"

"Ain't much tendin' to be done," Brinks said. "A bullet is the only treatment that makes sense."

"You ever set a bone before?"

"On a horse?"

"No," Hickok said.

Brinks rolled his eyes.

"Well, I've seen it done plenty," Brinks said. "I've helped set one or two, but I've never done it alone. Are you talking about your own self?"

Hickok stared at him.

Eight

Hickok knelt and placed his right arm on the stump, palm up. He was bare to the waist, and as he leaned forward Sarah Shull could count the ribs beneath his arm.

She knelt beside him and whispered in his ear, "Are you sure you want to do this, Jim?"

"I won't be worth a damn if I don't," he said sleepily.

Wellman wrapped a harness around Hickok's wrist. While Wellman pulled the harness tight, Brinks placed both of his hands on Hickok's forearm and probed roughly with his fingers.

Hickok flinched.

"Give him another round of dope," Brinks said.

Sarah produced another opium pill from the tiny bottle, but Hickok shook his head. She held the pill for a moment in her fingers, then placed it on her own tongue. Then she leaned in and kissed Hickok. As she did, she pushed the opium pill into his mouth.

Hickok was surprised, but swallowed.

"You boys didn't see a thing," Sarah said.

"He is relieved of both gun and knife?"

"The Colt is in the barn," Wellman said.

Sarah removed the knife from the leather scabbard that Hickok kept tucked into his belt. She handed the knife to Wellman, who threw it point-first into the ground behind him.

"If we're going to do this," Wellman said, "I think we are as set as we're ever going to be." He handed Brinks an ax handle, then braced himself against the harness attached to Hickok's wrist.

"Get his other hand," Brinks told Sarah.

She folded his left arm tight against his back, then locked her own arms around his and leaned into him. Hickok's face began to turn red.

"Not so tight yet," Brinks said. "I will start counting and find my spot. When I reach three, hold on tight. Understand? All right. One."

He ran his left hand over Hickok's forearm, feeling the break again.

"Two."

Brinks brought the ax handle forward and struck the forearm sharply. The sound of a snapping bone made Wellman's knees grow weak, and he nearly lost his grip as Hickok screamed and thrashed about.

"Doc, you sonuvabitch," Hickok said. "What happened to three?"

"Hold him," Brinks said. "We ain't to the hard part yet."

"Get off me," Hickok said. "Get away from me, you bitch of a succubus. Damn you, Doc, I'm going to kick your ass, and then I am going to beat Wellman to death with that harness."

Sarah placed her head against Hickok's neck.

"Be still, Jim," she said. "There's no turning back."

"Put something in his mouth," Brinks said.

Sarah wadded a kerchief and shoved it between his teeth.

"Don't swallow it," she said.

Although Hickok had been flushed only a few minutes before, now his skin felt cold to the touch.

"Get on with it," Wellman urged.

Brinks began to manipulate the bones in the arm. When he felt the ends scrape, Hickok jerked so violently that Sarah lost her grip on his left arm. He made a fist and blindly swung his arm in a wide arc, ending when his knuckles met Sarah's cheek.

Hickok spit out the kerchief and bellowed in rage. He tried to jerk away, but was stopped by the harness around his other wrist. His eyes rolled in the direction of the knife sticking into the ground a few yards away.

"Stop him before he runs the bones through his

skin," Sarah said, sitting on the ground and holding the right side of her face in both hands.

"Or before he gets the knife," Wellman said.

Brinks rapped the ax handle against Hickok's head.

Hickok collapsed over the stump, his body twitching.

"You've killed him," Sarah cried.

"His skull is too thick for that," Brinks said, wiping the sweat from his eyes with the tail of his shirt. He picked up Hickok's limp arm.

"Don't seem to be any extra holes," Brinks said as he pulled and twisted the arm into position. Then he glanced over at Sarah. "People will be remarking on that knot on the side of your face."

"To hell with them," she said.

"Somebody will have to tend him for a few days."

"I will," Sarah said. "What should I . . . I mean, when will we know?"

"A week," Brinks said. "He'll either get better in a hurry after that, or not. It's a clean break, so it shouldn't fester. I've heard surgeons say that pus is a good thing, but that's not my experience."

He began to splint the arm.

"Keep the bottle of dope," Brinks said. "He'll need it."

Nine

Hickok woke with a start.

"Go back to sleep," Sarah said.

Hickok blinked in the darkness. He could not place where they were. He was on his back, with his right arm on his stomach. Sarah's head was on his left shoulder.

Hickok looked around.

They were in the attic, and the door was open. The stars were shining, and the creek glistened with the light of the half-moon.

"Dream," Hickok mumbled.

"It's no dream," she said.

"No," Hickok said. "I mean I was having a dream. Christ, but I have a hangover."

"It's the dope," Sarah said.

"I was still a boy," Hickok said. "It was after Pa had died of the fever, and food was scarce.

Lorenzo was older and knew something about farming, but I was never much good at it. I spent most of my time in the woods, bringing game to the table. But hunting was just an excuse. Truth was, I preferred to be alone. It was easier than being around others and making small talk."

"Lorenzo," Sarah said. "Your brother?"

"One of them," Hickok said. "My favorite. He is the original Bill. For some damned reason, he took to calling himself Billy Barnes when were young. Probably some dime-novel foolishness. We shared a bed, and sometimes at night we'd talk. I must have asked him a thousand questions."

"About what?"

"About where folks go when they die," Hickok said. "I was having trouble digesting the idea that Pa was among us one day, and the next he was gone. I asked Lorenzo whether we'd ever see him again, like the preacher said. But Lorenzo said he didn't know. He said he wished he could believe it, and how he envied those that had faith. He allowed that it all was a mystery, and how it might be revealed to us after we're dead—or it might not."

"I believe in God," Sarah said.

"Why?"

"Because I know I'm going to hell," she said. "For hell to exist, there must be a God, even if He doesn't talk to me."

"You truly think you're going to hell?"

"And I reckon I will take a few with me," she said. "So . . . this dream. It doesn't sound that bad to be a child again. What disturbed you so?"

"It wasn't bad," Hickok said, "until Pa came back. I was in bed with Lorenzo and it was in the dead of night, and suddenly there was this awful sound and the house shook and Lorenzo and I flew to the window. Outside, the night sky had turned to blood and was shot through with lightning. Then the wind came up strong and blew open the front door downstairs. Lorenzo and I rushed down, and there was Pa standing in the doorway, fresh from the grave. His clothes were rags, and we could see bones poking through his flesh. I was terrified—I couldn't move nor speak. He pointed a bony finger and asked why I couldn't let him sleep."

"It was just a bad dream, James."

"Seemed pretty damned real to me," Hickok said.

"Childhood things dog us all of our lives," Sarah said.

"He called me his doubting son and said that I was doomed to wander the earth until I learned to long for death."

"That's cheerful," Sarah said.

"My arm hurts."

"My face hurts," Sarah said.

"Why?"

"You don't remember?" she said. "You hit me. Not on purpose, but with force enough."

"I'm sorry."

"No matter," she said. "It will heal. So will that arm, with a little luck. Will you finally tell me, my fair Jim, what caused the injury in the first place?"

Hickok smiled.

"I hear that it was a bear."

Sarah laughed.

"Tell me true," she said. "You owe me that."

"In Kansas I thought I was something, all right," Hickok said. "Scout. Hunter. Rode with some of the Free Staters in the border war. Nearly starved to death in the winter. Found a girl I thought I loved, but because she carried Indian blood my family thought it a poor match. They were right, I suppose. Drowned my heartache with whiskey and gambling. Then one day along the Smoky Hill I met a teamster by the name of Hackett, and he invited me to take a seat at his poker table. I knew he was a bully, and he mistook me for a young fool. We played for three days, taking breaks only to sleep a little, and in the end I cleaned him out. What a grand feeling it was. I'd never experienced anything like it. I felt nine feet tall. Then, as I was quitting the table with my fortune, Hackett accused me of cheating."

Hickok paused.

"And?"

"It happened right quick," he said. "I firmly but

quietly declared my innocence, but Hackett would have none of it. He kept bellowing about being cheated, and of course his friends took his side of it. I had no friends. Before I could reach for my gun, his fellows were upon me. They dragged me outside, and Hackett took great pleasure in breaking my arm over the rim of a wagon wheel."

"You settled the score, certainly."

"No," Hickok said. "I walked away broke and broken, and was lucky enough to receive a bit of charity from the stage company in the form of light duty. That's how I found myself here."

"And facing another bully."

"So it seems," Hickok said.

Something moved in the darkness in the yard below.

"There's someone out there," Hickok said.

"Pay no mind," Sarah said. "It is only McCanles's idiot son, Monroe. He is of the age where boys discover the sin of Onan, and he spies on me at night."

Ten

McCanles hitched his horse at the rail in front of the barn and looked over the station with disgust. It was the middle of July and he had not received a cent from the express company, and there was talk that the firm had gone bankrupt.

"Nice day?" Doc Brinks asked from the shade of the barn door.

"I can't say that it is," McCanles said. "I'm tired of the sight of this place. I have been waiting for months for payment, and all I have to show for it is a broken promise and a spread that looks like it is about to fall down."

"It could stand some work," Brinks agreed. "But things have been pitiful slow on the trail, and when things are slow the money just doesn't flow. Hell, I can't remember the last time I got paid."

A dog ran up, and Brinks knelt down to pet it.

"Now, there's a happy soul," Brinks said.

"Keep your hands away from my dog," Woods called. He and Gordon had just ridden into the yard. Monroe McCanles was behind them.

"Didn't know she was promised," Brinks said.

Gordon laughed.

"Shut up, you cross-eyed fool," Woods said.

"Clear out your trash," McCanles said. "As of today I am taking the station back and driving all of you squatters off."

"Where am I supposed to go?"

"It don't mean a damn to me," McCanles said. "But if I am not satisfied after speaking with the company superintendent in yonder house, I aim to burn the place to the ground. I'm quitting this country, and I'll be damned if I'm going to allow the company to have something of mine for nothing."

"That sounds a mite rash," Brinks said.

"If you are here in another ten minutes, you'll find out what rash really means," McCanles said. "My boys already have their orders, and only cash money will dissuade me."

Woods brought a box of matches from his pocket and shook them.

Brinks shook his head.

"Where's Duck Bill?"

"Up at the house, I reckon."

"Good," McCanles said. "I need to teach him

a lesson about sticking his beak where it don't belong."

"His arm's healed, Dave."

"Think that'll make a difference?"

Brinks shrugged.

"Monroe, fetch the kerosene from the barn and meet me up at the house," McCanles said.

Hickok was sitting at the table, drinking coffee with Wellman. Their conversation was interrupted when Sarah came in the open west door. She walked over to Hickok and placed a hand on his shoulder.

"McCanles," she said. "He's here. He's threatening to burn the station down if he doesn't get his money."

Wellman pushed himself away from the table, spilling the coffee in both cups.

"Sit down," Hickok said.

Hickok drew his revolver and handed it to Sarah.

"What are you doing?" Sarah asked.

"Place it on the bed behind the curtain," Hickok said.

"But why?"

"We should talk to him first, to discover his intentions. If he sees me sitting here armed, his first inclination won't be to talk."

"I told you what his intentions are," Sarah said. "I overheard him and Doc down at the barn. Unless you have his money, he plans to burn us out. Talking won't help."

"Are the two Jims with him?"

"Always," Sarah said.

"Put the Colt on the bed," Hickok said. When she had done so, he said, "Now get yourself outside and down into the cellar."

"I am not hiding in a cellar," Sarah said.

"Then sit over against the wall," Hickok said. "Keep quiet and don't move."

Hickok took another drink of coffee.

"Hello, there, in the house," McCanles called from the back door. "Wellman, are you in there?"

"He's here," Hickok called.

"Why, Duck Bill, how are you?" McCanles said. "I was hoping to find you here. I heard that you were all healed up and spoiling for mischief."

"I'm healed," Hickok said. "You know my name, and I would thank you to use it. What do you want, David McCanles?"

"Well, I have come to collect on the debt owed me by your employers, Russell, Majors, and Waddell, of the Central Overland California and Pikes Peak Express Company," McCanles said. "I have been gone on business for some time and was in hopes of obtaining the remaining two-thirds owed me, according to the terms of the contract. You see, I am anxious to settle all obligations due me before I depart this climate and offer my services to the Confederate States of America."

"You know we don't have the money," Wellman said.

"Now, I am disappointed to hear that," McCanles said. Monroe walked up behind his father. The boy was carrying a bucket of kerosene. "You remember Monroe, don't you? Oh, he certainly remembers you, Duck Bill. The boy has been telling me all about your nocturnal adventures. Why, good morning, Sarah—I almost missed you, what with you sitting so deep in the shadows."

"Go to hell, David."

"Ladies first," McCanles said. "But then, there ain't no ladies here, are there?"

There was a shriek from beyond the door, and McCanles turned just in time to ward off, with his right arm, a hoe swung by Jane Wellman.

The attack so surprised Monroe that he dropped the bucket of kerosene. It struck the hard ground in front of the doorway and sloshed over the threshold and drenched the boy's clothes.

"Hold on there," McCanles said, stepping toward her and taking the hoe away before she could swing it again. "You've been out in the garden a little too long, I'm afraid."

"You killed my father," she said, then spit in his face.

"Those are harsh words," McCanles said, grinning as he tossed the hoe into the yard. He withdrew a kerchief and wiped his face. "It wasn't my intention that the old man should die, just that he should quit stealing. I'm sorry for the former but glad of the latter."

"You are a lying piece of trash," Jane said. "Do you find it satisfying to abuse old men and women? Is that what pops your cap?"

He backhanded her across the mouth. She fell against the side of the house.

"I get no pleasure from it," McCanles said.

Wellman started to rise from his chair.

"Don't even think about it, Horace," McCanles called. He was looking at Jane, but he pointed a finger into the house. "I'll have my money now."

"There is no money," Hickok said.

"I'll have my satisfaction, then. You all clear out, because I aim to burn this place to the ground."

"This is company property, and I cannot let you do that," Hickok said.

"It is my property, and I insist," McCanles said.

Then he walked away from the back door, and Jane entered. She walked over and took a seat next to Sarah.

"Jane, are you all right?" Wellman asked.

"The sonuvabitch hit me," she said. "Do you think I'm all right?"

"Now what?" Wellman asked, leaning across the table.

"We wait."

"For what? The fire to start chafing our butts?"

"What are you boys whispering about in there?" McCanles asked, now appearing at the steps beyond the open side door. "Do you mind if I come in?"

"We'd prefer you didn't," Horace said.

"Say, it is powerful warm out here," McCanles said. "I see your water basin right here by the door. Would you spare a parched soul a drink of water?"

Hickok rose from the table and scooped a cup of water from the basin. He handed it to McCanles, who took a sip. His eyes never left Hickok.

"Are you thirsty as well?" Hickok asked Monroe.

"He can have my water," McCanles said, and passed the tin cup to his son.

The boy took the cup and drank.

"You'd better get his clothes changed," Hickok said. "He reeks of coal oil. It will burn his skin. He is liable to ignite if he comes near an open flame."

"Giving fatherly advice now, are we?" McCanles asked. He laughed as he drew a pipe from the pocket of his coat and casually filled it with tobacco. Then he patted down his pockets. "I seem to have left my lucifers with the two Jims. Do you mind if I come in and light a twig from the fireplace?"

"I gave you water," Hickok said. "I draw the line at fire. Does the boy have any spare clothes?"

"Can't say we brought any," McCanles said. "Thought this would be a short trip."

"Then let the women clean him up."

"The Jims will take care of it later."

"The boy's uncomfortable," Hickok said. "Monroe, do you want to come in and get out of those oily things?"

Monroe stared at Hickok.

"Do you talk?"

"He talks to me," McCanles said. "Don't you, son? We talk about all manner of things. He is at the age, you understand, when a boy has a powerful curiosity about certain mysteries. But I reckon you have taught him all about that, by example."

"Better mine than yours," Hickok said.

"Ah," McCanles said. "Found a match."

He withdrew the match from his pocket and held it up.

The boy backed away.

"No more nonsense," Hickok said. "Do not strike that match."

"And if I do?"

"You've had your warning," Hickok said.

Hickok stepped toward the back of the house. He nodded to Wellman, who rose from the table and followed him. Hickok ducked behind the blanket that separated the beds from the rest of the room, picked up his revolver and put it in its holster, then took the Hawken rifle from the wall. Wellman retrieved an old dragoon revolver from beneath the bed.

"Be ready," Hickok said. "The others will come when they hear the shooting."

"What happened to talking?"

"The time for words is over."

Hickok stepped out from behind the blanket with the rifle at his cheek. He drew the hammer back with his thumb.

McCanles was standing in the sunlight and could not see into the shadows within the house. But he heard the sound of the rifle being cocked, and he reached for his pistol.

Hickok fired.

He dropped the rifle and drew the Colt with his right hand, walking in a crouch through the haze of black powder smoke. His ears rang with the sound of the shot.

McCanles was sprawled on his back in the yard, his hat beside him. The .50-caliber ball had struck him squarely in the chest. His eyes were open, and blood trickled from his nostrils.

Monroe was kneeling beside his father. He had his father's gun, a .44-caliber Remington revolver, in his lap.

The boy stared at Hickok with hate.

"You killed him," he said.

"Yes," Hickok said.

With both hands, the boy thrust the barrel of the Remington toward Hickok.

"Why?"

"It was necessary," Hickok said.

The barrel wavered.

Hickok heard Wellman coming up behind, and he motioned for him to stand down.

"Sons of bitches," the boy said, tears streaming down his cheeks. He blinked, trying to keep the gun sighted on Hickok's chest.

"They're coming," Wellman said.

Hickok stepped toward the boy. He reached down and placed his hand over the gun. The boy's finger twitched on the trigger.

"Next time you'll probably want to cock it," Hickok said as he drew the gun away.

They went back into the house. Hickok motioned for Wellman to watch the back door, while he took the side. Seconds later Woods stepped through the back doorway, revolver drawn.

Wellman fired.

Woods dropped the gun. He stumbled into the yard, clutching his stomach.

Gordon, who was kneeling beside the body of David McCanles, heard the shot. He got to his feet and, with a shotgun in his hand, peered through the side door.

Hickok drew the Navy and fired.

The bullet shattered Gordon's lower jaw.

Gordon dropped the shotgun and fell to the ground. He held the bottom half of his face with both hands, blood dripping between his fingers. Then he got to his feet and lurched toward the brush behind the house.

Woods was crawling along the side of the house. Jane Wellman was behind him. She had retrieved the grubbing hoe from where McCanles had thrown it.

Woods looked behind, saw the woman with the hoe, and tried frantically to crawl faster. Jane lifted the hoe and brought it down with all of her strength on the back of his head.

"This is what we do to snakes," she said.

She pulled the blade free and repeated the process until her shoulders were tired and her face and arms were splattered with blood.

"Where's Gordon?" Wellman asked as he picked the shotgun from the ground.

"Crawled off into the brush," Hickok said.

They heard a dog yapping and followed the sound into the thicket. They found Gordon huddled on his side, trying to shoo the dog away.

Wellman raised the shotgun.

"Don't kill me," Gordon pleaded.

"Why, you cross-eyed son of a bitch," Wellman said. He pulled the trigger, and the buckshot took away the top of Gordon's head. Then he turned and emptied the other barrel into the dog.

When they returned to the house, they found Brinks standing between Jane and the boy. Jane's bloody hands gripped the hoe.

"Go away, Doc," she said. "This one has to die as well."

"He's just a boy," Brinks said.

"They're just as deadly when they're small."

"Then what?" Brinks asked. "After you slay this

one, are you going to the home of the widow McCanles and killing her and the rest of the children?"

"No," Jane said, blinking. "Of course not."

"Go home, boy," Brinks said.

Monroe scrambled away.

"Are any of you hurt?" Brinks asked.

"No," Hickok said.

"Which of them fired first?" Brinks said.

"None of them," Hickok said.

"Then how—"

"We kept the advantage," Hickok said.

"It was murder, then," Brinks said.

"They meant the same for us."

Hickok turned to see Sarah hugging the body of David McCanles. She seemed to be shaking him, or crying—Hickok could not tell because her back was to him. He handed the empty shotgun to Wellman, walked over, and placed a hand on her shoulder.

She turned. Her green eyes were wild and her dark hair clung to her forehead. She released her grip on the collar of the coat and McCanles slumped away. In her bloodstained right hand was a bag of gold coins.

Hickok never saw her again.

Eleven

Hickok stepped from the shadows of the Bailey House into the sunshine of South Street. He had spent most of the past three days drinking and playing cards in an upstairs room of the hotel. He had slept little and eaten less, and his eyes burned from the glare of the busy street, which was filled with wagons, merchants, and soldiers.

"Jim!" a voice called.

Hickok blinked.

"James!"

One of the wagons drew to a stop a few paces away, and the wheels rocked backward as the mule team shuffled nervously. The driver threw the reins to his partner and jumped down into the mud.

"Lorenzo," Hickok said.

His older brother hugged him, pinning his

arms, and lifted him into the air. When Lorenzo released him, Hickok threw an uppercut that narrowly missed his brother's nose but knocked his hat into the street.

"Careful there, pathfinder," Lorenzo said.

"You be careful yourself, Lorenzo."

The older man held a finger to his lips.

"They know me as Bill out here," he said.

"That damned nickname again," Hickok said. "That's a problem, for that's what they call me as well. Perhaps you should call me Jim."

"Nobody goes by their given names on the frontier," Lorenzo scolded. "But it will be no trouble. You can be Little Bill."

"I would rather be Great Bill," Hickok said.

"We will wrestle for it," Lorenzo said.

"Later, for I'm afraid I am nearly too drunk to stand."

"Ha!" Lorenzo cried. "I knew it. I will have to lie in my letters to Mother, however. I trust that you will eventually redeem my lies, no?"

"I've found that war is a great demoralizer."

"What are you doing here? The last word I had from you was that they had you up on murder charges in Nebraska Territory. I must admit you had me worried, little brother."

"The court released me," Hickok said. "There was an inquiry, but the testimony was equivocal."

"Let's hope your luck holds."

"It didn't, at least not in the poker game

upstairs," Hickok said. "I'm afraid I've lost my last dollar. I'm here looking for work, and was hoping that you could assist me."

"I can get you a job on a wagon."

"If needed," Hickok said, then coughed. "I was hoping for something that required more brains and less muscle. The army is seeking scouts, no?"

"Always," Lorenzo said. "But the scouts employed here serve more as spies than in blazing trails or killing game. Does that deter you?"

"Should it?"

"It would any sane man," Lorenzo said.

"Then I don't see the problem."

Lorenzo laughed.

"No, I guess you wouldn't," he said. "Personally, I am satisfied to drive freight between here and Rolla. The railroad has not yet made it here, and the army is sorely in need of every kind of supply. The pay is good and the risks are common ones. But I know a few people here, and will make a discreet investigation."

Hickok nodded.

"In the meantime, I have to get this freight delivered," Lorenzo said. "Are you staying at this hotel?"

"I was."

Lorenzo dug into the pocket of his trousers and brought out a few coins, which he pressed into his brother's hand.

"A loan?"

"Consider it a gesture of fraternal affection," Lorenzo said. "Square yourself with the hotel, and for God's sake, buy yourself dinner. You are even thinner than I remembered. No poker until you are flush, agreed?"

"Is the lecture a gift as well?"

"Damn you," Lorenzo said, laughing. He picked up his hat from the ground and climbed back into the seat of the wagon. "Stay close. I will call for you tonight, and you can tell me of the trouble at Rock Creek."

"Nothing to tell," Hickok said.

"Ha!" Lorenzo said, then released the brake and urged the team. He called over his shoulder, "Watch your back."

"Watch yours," Hickok said.

Hickok weighed the coins in his hand as he watched the wagon roll away. Then he slipped the money into his coat pocket, walked back into the hotel, and climbed the stairs to the eternal poker game on the second floor.

Twelve

Hickok placed his cards on the table.

"Full house, gentlemen," he said. The three other players at the table groaned as Hickok raked in the pot. "Sorry, but the cards seem to favor me tonight."

"Mind if I sit in?" a deep voice called from the back of the room. "I hear this is the best poker game in town, and I know something about poker."

Hickok recognized the voice, but he did not look up as he tucked the money into his vest pocket.

"Help yourself," a dry-goods merchant said as he left his chair. "I hope your luck is better than mine. The feller with the money has been on a streak all day."

"Streaks are made to be broken," the big man

said as he took the chair. He was dressed in the work clothes of a teamster.

"I will sit this hand out," Hickok said. He picked up the whiskey bottle from the table and carefully refilled his glass.

"Already feel like your luck has run out, eh?"

"No," Hickok said, taking a shot of whiskey.

"Then what?"

"I don't play with your kind."

The room fell silent.

"I don't believe I heard you right," the teamster said, placing his forearms on the table.

"You heard me right."

"Then just what do you mean by my kind?"

Hickok refilled the glass, drained it, and placed it upon the table.

"Liars," he said.

The other players backed away from the table.

"Now, is that any way to treat a stranger?" the teamster asked. "We've only known each other for a few moments and you are throwing some ugly words around. Before I bust you up, tell me what you mean."

"You don't remember me."

"Why should I?"

Hickok smiled.

"Your name is Hackett," he said. "We played some cards once in Kansas Territory. I was winning and you couldn't stand it, so you accused me of cheating, and then you and your friends dragged me outside and broke my arm over a wagon wheel."

"I'll be damned," the teamster said. "You are that little runt. I should have recognized that beak of yours. And you were cheating."

The teamster stood up, but Hickok remained seated.

"Boys," Hickok said to the other gamblers, "have you ever known me to cheat?"

"No, never," the dry-goods merchant said.

"Or to lie?"

They all agreed to the negative.

"You skinny sonuvabitch," the teamster said. He grabbed the edge of the table and tossed it aside, spilling cards and whiskey on the floor— and revealing Hickok's revolver, which was casually held in his left hand.

The teamster stopped.

"You don't seem to be wearing a gun, but I'll wager you have a weapon on you somewhere," Hickok said. "Find it and slowly place it on the floor."

"Go to hell," Hackett said.

Hickok drew the hammer back with his thumb.

The teamster held his hands up, then slowly reached inside his shirt and, with two fingers, withdrew a one-shot pocket pistol.

"On the floor."

Hackett knelt and placed the pistol on the floor.

"You're going to shoot me, unarmed? That's murder."

"What you did to me wasn't exactly within the law," Hickok said. "Stand up."

The teamster rose.

"I'm sorry," he said. "It was a misunderstanding. If you say you weren't cheating, then I believe you."

"An apology at the point of a gun is meaningless," Hickok said. "I could ask you to sing 'The Star-Spangled Banner' and tell me that my real father is the king of France and you would."

Hickok lowered the hammer on the revolver, placed it on the floor beside the chair, and then rose.

"Now I want you to apologize."

"You're dumber than I thought," Hackett said, then rushed forward. He threw a right, and Hickok blocked it with his left, then drove his own right hand into the teamster's ribs.

Hackett gasped, but seized Hickok by the front of the shirt, spun around, and pinned him against the wall. He hit him once in the face and then drove a knee upward, but Hickok turned his body and took the blow on his leg. He shoved his thumbs into Hackett's eyes.

The teamster bellowed and staggered backward.

Hickok kicked him in the stomach, driving him through the doorway and onto the second-story balcony. As Hickok came out after him, Hackett pulled a knife from his boot and slashed wildly. Hickok jumped out of the reach of the blade, then picked up a wooden chair that was on the porch and swung it at Hackett.

The chair broke over the teamster's head, and the knife slipped from his hand. As soon as it clattered to the floor, Hickok kicked it over the side of the porch.

Hackett snatched up a leg of the broken chair and advanced toward Hickok. He swung twice, and each time Hickok dodged the blow. Hackett was panting now, and his third swing lacked the power of the first two. Hickok grasped the teamster's wrist with both hands and rolled backward, bringing the teamster off his feet, and threw him against the rail.

The rail broke and Hackett went over.

When he landed on the hard-packed dirt of the street below, it drove the breath from his lungs. He lay gasping for a few moments, unable to draw air. When he finally was able to take a breath, he clutched his chest and rolled onto his side in pain.

"You've broken my ribs." He gasped.

"It's less than you deserve," Hickok called from the balcony as he brushed the dust from his clothes.

The owner of the hotel appeared in the doorway of the balcony, enraged.

"Who's going to pay for this mess?"

"If life were fair, it would be the man on the ground whimpering about his ribs," Hickok said. He took the money from his vest pocket and held it out. "I'm sure this is more than enough to pay for the damages, and I have to say, it was worth every dime."

Thirteen

Hickok ducked beneath the flap of the tent and stood next to his brother. The officer at the field desk did not look up from his book.

Lorenzo cleared his throat.

The officer held up a forefinger and continued reading.

Hickok exchanged looks with Lorenzo, who shrugged.

In a few minutes, the officer closed the book and placed it on the desk. Then he removed his wire-frame glasses and placed them atop the book.

"Your brother?" the officer asked.

"Yes, sir," Lorenzo said.

"Aren't there any short folks in your family?"

"No, sir."

The officer smiled.

"What's your name, son?"

"James Butler," Hickok said. "But my friends call me Bill."

"So you're both called Bill?"

"That's right," Hickok said. "But I'm the wild one."

"Wild Bill?"

"Yes, sir."

Lorenzo's eyes blazed.

"So that would make you Tame Bill," the officer remarked.

"I reckon it would," Lorenzo said.

"Very well," the officer said. "Wild Bill, I understand that you are seeking employment as a scout. I am John Kelso, and I am the one to grant your wish, if you are a good fit."

"I am used to dealing with rough men," Hickok said.

"Not what I had in mind," the officer said. "In your desired line of work, folks live longer by doing more thinking and less fighting. Now, turn around."

"Pardon?"

"You heard me. Show me your back."

Hickok turned.

"Am I wearing glasses?"

"Not now."

"How old am I?"

"Thirty," Hickok said. "A little older, perhaps."

"My rank?"

"Captain."

"Am I armed? Consider all options."

"You aren't carrying on your person, unless it is hidden," Hickok said. "On the desk is a penknife, which would make a poor weapon. Behind you, hanging from a peg, is a carbine. It's capped. There's a lantern on the table and it is smoking something fierce. The wick needs trimming."

Kelso smiled.

"All right, we'll go on to something a little harder," Kelso said. "Tell me the title and the author of the book I was reading."

"Henry David Thoreau," Hickok said. "'*Civil Disobedience' and Other Essays.* I know the book, sir."

"Oh?" Kelso asked. "What did you think of it?"

"I liked what he had to say about how the best governments govern the least," Hickok said. "But I did not care for his pacifism. Seems to me that action is needed to correct evil. The peaceful stuff didn't seem to square with what Mr. Thoreau wrote later about how John Brown was in the right at Harpers Ferry."

"So, you're a scholar as well?"

"No, sir," Hickok said. "We were raised with all this stuff that came out of Boston. Our folks ran a stop on the Underground for runaway slaves, and Mother read aloud to us from Thoreau and the others. Guess you could call it our religion."

Kelso laughed.

"The last thing I would have expected to run

into was a scout versed in transcendentalism," he said. "You may turn around, Mr. Hickok."

Hickok turned as gracefully as a dancer.

"You know how to use that thing on your hip?"

"With either hand."

"You have a horse?"

"He will by morning," Lorenzo said.

"Used to taking care of your little brother?"

"James . . . I mean Wild Bill has been out west for a few years now and has made a good account of taking care of himself."

"That is good, for he will have to take care of himself very well indeed," Kelso said. "If you will excuse us, I have some matters to discuss with your brother."

Lorenzo nodded, then slipped out of the tent.

Hickok drew a cigar from his pocket.

"Don't plan on lighting that thing in here," Kelso said. "I disapprove of the use of tobacco, coffee, and strong drink. Swearing is discouraged, and improper behavior with females will not be tolerated. Do you understand?"

"Perfectly," Hickok said. He removed the cigar from his mouth and returned it to his pocket.

"Draw near," Kelso said as he spread a map on the table. "To be effective, you must understand the present situation and know what to look for. You know how to read a map?"

"Of course," Hickok said. "This is southern Missouri and northern Arkansas. We're here—that's

Springfield. This is the road leading to Rolla and beyond, all the way to St. Louis. Here are the two roads leading to Arkansas: the coach road to Forsyth and the Wire Road, which follows the old White River Trace going to Fayetteville."

"Good," Kelso said. "Now, Claiborne Jackson and his rebels have beaten Nathaniel Lyon and his Dutch at Carthage, over in Jasper County, and that has given them some advantage. In the bigger battle to come, they will be firing lead at us taken from the mines near Granby."

"How long before this battle?"

"A fortnight, at most," Kelso said. "Sterling Price has been joined by Ben McCulloch from Texas, and a number of volunteers from Louisiana. We are likely to meet a force of ten or twelve thousand."

"Damn," Hickok mused. "Sorry, sir. What is our strength?"

"We don't know," Kelso said. "Lyon escaped all but intact from Carthage, but a number of his men enlisted for only three months, and that time is up. Many of the men, and a fair number of the officers, have already left. It is anybody's guess how many will remain when the fight is joined."

"So the fight will be for Springfield?"

"No, this is just where the fight will take place—or somewhere nearby. If we lose, of course, Springfield will be taken by the enemy. But what we are fighting for is control of northern Arkansas, and that is where I want you to go. There are a number of locations of strategic importance within a few days' ride, such as the saltpeter mine near Yellville. You know why saltpeter is important?"

"You can't make gunpowder without it," Hickok said.

"That is the trouble," Kelso said. "Most of the nation's resources are being expended, and rightly so, east of the Mississippi. Here on the frontier, the struggle will be over who controls the means to fight, the arsenals and stores and mines."

"And my role?"

"To infiltrate the rebel lines and report back on their positions, their possessions, and their weaknesses," Kelso said.

"How best to do that?"

"Ordinarily, a stranger in these wild hills of Arkansas wouldn't last until sundown," Kelso said. "These Arkansawyers are a clannish and distrustful lot. But since the arrival of thousands of Texans and Louisianians, there is an opportunity for someone who speaks and acts a bit differently to slip in and back out unmolested, as long as his story seems credible."

"What is my story?"

"That will be a matter of enterprise and opportunity," Kelso said. "As the battle draws nigh onto Springfield, I want you to scout the enemy positions. Study their manner of dress, their organization, and their rituals. When the shooting starts, exploit whatever opening presents itself to get behind the enemy lines and assume a new identity. Your life will depend on your ability to weave a convincing story. Your personality and lack of military service will be an advantage in this, because the rebels have little discipline or regard for authority."

Hickok nodded.

"You will go without papers and without hope of rescue, should you find yourself distressed," Kelso said. "Upon your return, you will be admitted back into my company only when you utter the appropriate password."

"What is the password?"

"There are a number of passwords," Kelso said. "Some of them change daily, and you shall not be privy to these. You will have to make your way back into our lines as best you can. But once inside, the commanding officers are under orders to bring those who speak special passwords directly to me so they may report."

Kelso folded the map.

"Your password," he said, "is Thoreau."

Fourteen

Hickok placed the stirrup over the saddle, then ducked beneath the belly of the horse to grab the end of the cinch strap.

"A little light," he said.

Lorenzo took the candle lantern down from the post and held it low. His brother's eyes were puffy and bloodshot, and he could smell the whiskey on his breath.

"Now, don't you engage in any heroics," Lorenzo said. "This fight is already lost. Lyon has only five thousand men, maybe less. Your dying won't change a thing."

"I don't aim to die, at least not yet," Hickok said as he tightened the cinch. "Any word on the reinforcements from St. Louis?"

"There are no reinforcements coming," Lorenzo

said. "The command in St. Louis has decided to abandon Springfield to its fate."

"I don't like that kind of talk," Hickok said.

"Like it or lump it, but it won't change the odds," Lorenzo said. "As soon as you ride out, I'm going to make tracks for Rolla."

Hickok stood.

"You have everything you need?" Lorenzo asked.

"Yes," Hickok said. "I thank you for the horse. I will call him Mazeppa, for *The Wild Horse of Tartary.*"

"He already has a name," Lorenzo said. "You can't go changing the name of a horse. It confuses them. Why does everything have to be a little bit bigger than life with you, Jim?"

Hickok ignored the question.

"He's a fine animal and will bring me back safely," he said at last.

"I depend on it."

"Don't go soft on me," Hickok said brightly. "Why, the war will probably be over by the time I get back from holiday in Arkansas."

Hickok clasped his brother's hand.

"Farewell, Jim," Lorenzo said.

Hickok nodded.

"I don't expect to post any letters for a spell," he said. "Write a few lines to Mother on my behalf."

Fifteen

The dark streets of Springfield were slick with rain as Hickok left the stable behind and urged his horse down the Wire Road toward the southwest. The rain had stopped, but the moon—nearly in its first quarter—was shrouded in storm clouds. Here and there a candle flickered in the midnight darkness, and voices in low tones carried in the stillness. He had muffled the hooves of the horse in burlap, and if his passage was noticed, it stirred no interest.

He left the city behind and followed the Wire Road to Grand Prairie. After mounting a series of low hills, he came to a spot overlooking Wilson Creek. Below him, on the east bank, the fires of a Confederate camp glittered in the dark. He watched for several minutes, but could discern no activity. There were few tents, and most of the men seemed to be sleeping on the steep banks of the creek. Now and then one of them would shift in their rocky bed and Hickock could see the glint of starlight from the barrel of a weapon. Finally he turned his horse to the west and left the road for the tall grass.

A quarter of a mile farther on, he picked up the creek again and crossed. The water was shallow and full of stones, which clattered beneath the weight of horse and rider. As he was walking the horse onto the opposite bank, he heard the double click of a rifle hammer being cocked.

"Who goes there?"

"Scout," Hickok said.

There was no reply.

"Union scout," Hickok said.

"How do I know?"

"Skirmishers don't ride alone," Hickok said.

He could see the outline of the picket now, just outside the timber that came to the edge of the creek, not twenty yards away. The muzzle of the big rifle had a bayonet fixed to the end, and was pointed at Hickok.

"You fire that piece," Hickok said, "and you'll alert all the rebels downstream of our intentions. Would you like to do that?"

"No," the picket said. He hesitantly lowered the Springfield, then gently thumbed down the hammer.

"Good lad," Hickok said.

"I thought you were the entire Southern army riding across the creek," the boy said. "Mister, you scared the hell out of me.

"You returned the compliment."

The boy took off his cap and wiped his sleeve across his forehead. His hair was the color of wheat.

"Did you see them?" he asked.

"Yes," Hickok said.

"Are there as many as they say?"

"It is difficult to make an estimate in the darkness," Hickok said. "But there are thousands."

The boy nodded.

"I imagine you'll want to talk to those that wear the swords," he said. "Straight up the hill." The boy saluted.

Hickok paused. He had never been saluted before, and was unsure of his rank—or even if he had one. He tugged on the reins of his horse and said, "Don't do that, boy. You just might get me shot as an officer."

As Hickok rode up the hill, it began to rain. He walked the horse through the lines of soldiers who were either sleeping or huddled in clusters, talking in low tones. He dismounted near a group of tents, and before his boots had touched the ground a corporal had appeared from the shadows to take his reins.

"Keep him close," Hickok said.

The corporal nodded.

A small fire burned in a circle of rocks not far from the tents, and over the fire hung a coffeepot. A couple of men were sitting on logs, facing the fire, and Hickok walked over and asked if he could share their coffee.

The firelight reflected in their eyes as they looked up.

"It is about the sorriest excuse for coffee I have tasted in a long while," said one of the men. He wore a rather elaborate uniform, with a double row of brass buttons, and Hickok recognized the insignia of a major.

The other man was silent. He was small in stature, with wild hair and a thin beard, and he wore a rather well-worn uniform that might have suited a captain.

Hickok took the tin cup the major offered and, using a kerchief taken from a back pocket, carefully tipped the pot to fill the cup.

"It must be the water here," the major said.

"Pardon?"

"The coffee," he continued. "It takes on the flavor of the water from which it is made. The water from the creek has a peculiar taste, at least to my palate." The man looked up at the night sky. "It is beginning to rain harder now. Perhaps we should catch some of the rainwater so as to make some decent coffee. I have a rubber blanket here we could catch some in easily enough. What do you think, Nate?"

"No," the man in the plain uniform said. "We have bigger things to worry about than coffee. And by noontime, I'll wager, the water of that bitter creek will taste sweet indeed."

Hickok sat on a stump and used the kerchief to hold the tin cup, to keep from burning his hands. The rain was drumming on the brim of his slouch hat.

The major unrolled the waterproof bedroll and handed it to the other man, who draped it around his shoulders.

"You aren't a soldier," the major observed. "Do you reside near here? A farmer, perhaps?"

"He's no farmer," the small man said. "He has the look of the far West about him. I've seen it often enough. . . . I've employed many of his kind as scouts and trailblazers. And, on occasion, murderers."

"I'm a scout," Hickok said quietly.

"Are you a murderer?" the small man asked.

"I have killed men," Hickok said, "but I found no pleasure in it. A judge decided that it was not murder, but that was simply the law of man. If you were to ask a higher authority, you might get a different answer."

"Be careful, son," the major said. "In the fight to come, your conscience may get you killed. You must not hesitate to slay the enemy when the opportunity presents itself."

"Leave the boy alone, John."

"But, Nate—"

"I know of which I speak," the man said, the firelight dancing in his hollow eyes. "In California, some years ago, I slaughtered four hundred savages—men, women, and children. It was in retaliation for the killing of two settlers, men of no real consequence, but white men nonetheless. I found out later that I had the wrong Indians. Of course, the sacrificial Indians were not without blame, I now suppose, and had committed uncounted atrocities against our race, but still . . . they writhe and die now in my dreams, braves with Stone Age tools against powder and ball, and mothers with babes in arms."

"It was unpleasant," Hickok said, anxious to change the subject. "But a soldier's duty."

"A soldier's duty is to die," the man said. "An officer's duty is to send them to their deaths. And no, it wasn't battle. I've seen battle—in Mexico, me and the other fools that graduated from West Point. Now here we are again, but we're not fighting foreigners. We're going to fight each other, from the Potomac to this little patch of desolation known as . . . what is it?"

"Grand Prairie," the major said.

"Yes, that's it. But God knows what history will call it. It will go by different names, depending on what side you're on. As the fighting progresses, a landmark will be chosen, one of these hills or perhaps the creek, which will roll gloriously from the tongue without offending the soul."

The major pulled a flask from his pocket.

"Take a nip of this," he said. "You need some cheer."

The other man pushed it aside.

"Save it for later," he said.

"You speak as if all is lost," the major said. "The day will hold many surprises, and you must retain your confidence to take full advantage."

"All certainly is lost," the man said bitterly. "Fremont, the great pathfinder, has revealed himself to be nothing more than a coward and a fool. His inaction has turned what promised to be a decisive victory into a meaningless sacrifice. With support, we could have crushed McCulloch and his Army of the West. Instead, we are serving him victory on a platter of the finest silver."

"If I may, sir," Hickok said.

"Speak your mind."

"Surely there is honor in defending an ideal."

"Of which ideal do you speak, youth?"

"Of freedom," he said. "For all men. The liberation of the dark race, sir."

The man grimaced.

"Not another bloody abolitionist."

"Well, yes," Hickok said. "Sir."

"The problem with the niggers," he said, "is that they are no better than us. The only difference is that our burden is greater."

"Begging the gentleman's pardon," Hickok said, "but the burden of captivity is somewhat greater."

"If you survive long enough, son, age will rob you of your ideals," he said. "It will chip away at them, one by one. It will begin with the sad realization that your parents and your preacher, if you are of a religious bent, are but vessels made of inferior workmanship—no better and no worse than you yourself. But somehow, it is easier to overlook the faults in oneself than in those we respect. We can lie and tell ourselves that our true nature is much nobler than we have allowed it to be, that tomorrow we will make amends and let our lights shine brightly, and that for just today we will forgive ourselves. But others . . . there's the rub. Not being privy to their innermost thoughts, we must judge them solely upon actions and not intentions. And all come up short. Even those who sin not seem lacking. We are suspicious of those who are too good. Are not such creatures merely a product of a scarcity of opportunity? What a comfort these thoughts are when we are confronted by our betters. And what peace in laying our heads upon our soiled pillows and banking on that eternal tomorrow. And in the end—do you know what this unbroken line of corruption leads to?"

"I reckon you're going to tell me," Hickok said.

"It leads to the unpleasant discovery that all of your tomorrows are gone. My chances at redemption are all used up, for I will not live to see the sunset."

"You don't know that," the major gently scoffed.

"But I do," the man said. "I have seen a great many things in my dreams during the past few nights. Along with those anguished savages have been glimpses of my own death, my body abandoned on the field of battle."

"Your men would never let that happen."

The man smiled.

"Oh, but it will," he said. "I have also seen your death, John Schofield, many years from now—by your own device, no less."

"Nonsense," the major said.

"Do not despair, John. You have much of life ahead, and how I envy that."

Hickok sipped his coffee.

"General," he said. "You have given up before the battle has even started."

"Do not worry, scout," the strange man said, and smiled. "I will not die a coward's death. I will be the first general officer to fall in battle, and I will fight like a demon and make McCulloch pay dearly for his triumph. All I ask is that my body be returned to Connecticut for burial. I am rather melancholy to think of my bones bleaching on this windswept prairie."

"Should you fall," the major said, "I promise."

"Fair enough."

"Let us speak no more of death," Hickok said, and threw the rest of his coffee into the fire, where it billowed into steam. "My orders are to cross the lines and slip into Arkansas, but if there is anything I can do to help you while accomplishing that, sir, I stand ready."

"Scout, your primary job is to stay alive," he said. "You'll do that by reasoning and not by might. The rebel guns are arranged out there in the darkness, their hungry muzzles only a few hundred yards away, and that is your primary obstacle. When first light comes, they will open up on anything they see moving in the netherland between us. We will attempt to keep the high ground, on Oak Hill yonder, so as to gain some type of advantage."

Hickok nodded.

"Once you are behind their lines, you must avoid the Fayetteville road, because that will lead you into the teeth of Sigel's position. Strike out on the prairie in a westerly direction to avoid the Dutch—unless you speak German. Don't look back."

"Thank you for the coffee," Hickok said. "And your counsel."

"It seems the rain is slackening," the major said.

"And the sky is glowing with the promise of dawn," the other said. "It is time, John, for us to rouse the men and to prepare for what is to come."

He threw off the bedroll and stood.

"What is your name, scout?"

"My family name is Hickok, but they call me Wild Bill."

"Store up some tomorrows, Wild Bill," he said. "Hang on to your unblemished ideals for as long as possible. Forget the ravings of an old man. Live well, find a woman you can trust, and hang up your guns when this war is done."

"A pretty thought," Hickok said.

"Make it true," the man said.

Sixteen

As Lyon's men advanced, Hickok rode some distance behind. The army moved slowly, steadily, like some lumbering animal seeking out its prey in the half-light of dawn. Everywhere were the sound of creaking leather and the metallic rasp of bayonets and the hollow sound of canteens thumping against rifle stocks, and above all the curious thrumming sound of a thousand soldiers making their way through the prairie grass.

Hickok's chest was tight, and on the tip of his tongue he tasted something acrid that might have been fear. He forced himself to breathe, and he could smell wood smoke and leather and sweat. All battles, he thought, must have smelled and felt and tasted like this in those precious few minutes before they were joined—masses of men with murderous intent moving unspeaking through morning haze, their legs wet with morning dew, white knuckles upon their weapons, their hearts in their throats.

As he rode forward his fear gave way to excitement, and he was seized by a sudden and unexpected exuberance. There were more men here than this otherwise commonplace stretch of prairie had ever known. He felt pride in being a part of such a vast undertaking, and he was sorry for any man unfortunate enough never to have experienced it. Lost in his thoughts, swept along in the wake of the army, and allowing his horse to pick the easiest terrain, he allowed himself to be drawn to the east, toward the creek bottom, instead of in the direction he had been advised to follow. He realized his mistake when he reached the water's edge. Ahead of him, the soldiers were rushing now through a cornfield toward the enemy camps. The Confederates managed a few scattered shots, but these were answered in force by the advancing Union troops.

There were shouting and anguished screams, and then the hillsides all around him seemed to erupt at once with rifle fire. A curious buzzing sound puzzled Hickok and reminded him of insects, but then he turned in the saddle and saw branches of the trees in the woods behind being felled by the large rifle balls that filled the air. As he leaned low over the neck of his horse and began to turn the animal back toward the safety of the tree line, there were three brilliant flashes on the hillside across the creek. Two of the shells exploded in the ranks of men ahead, throwing bodies and cornstalks high into the air, and the third erupted at the top of an oak tree behind him.

Only then did he hear the sound of the cannon blasts, which rolled down the creek bottom like thunder. His horse bucked and reared, and Hickok struggled to stay in the saddle. Then there was another bright flash from the far hillside, another shell exploded in the trees, and the horse raced forward, across the creek. The horse topped the rocky hillside, and Hickok found himself in the middle of what a few minutes before had been one of the rebel camps. A dozen bodies clad in homespun clothes littered the ground, along with their hats and rifles and bedrolls, and scraps of paper drifted on the morning breeze—newspapers, letters home, paper money. Everything seemed to be moving in slow motion as Hickok attempted to get the horse reined in and moving in the opposite direction.

The Confederates had retreated to a rocky ledge some hundred yards away. Around the ruined camp, squads of Union soldiers had taken cover in ditches and behind trees and rail fences.

"What in hell do you think you're doing?" a sergeant called from behind a fence corner. "Get down before you get your head blown off."

A homespun-clad soldier rose from the ground and grasped the bridle with a bloody hand.

"Let go," Hickok said.

The wounded rebel's shoes scraped the ground as the nervous horse backed away. With the reins bunched in his left fist, Hickok drew a revolver with his right hand and pointed it to the ground.

"Damn you," Hickok said.

"Kill him," the sergeant shouted.

Hickok hesitated.

The sergeant brought his rifle to his shoulder and fired.

The shot took away the back of the rebel's head, and a long moment later the bridle slipped from his fingers. He fell heavily to the ground and rolled once, his vacant eyes to the sky and a cocked single-shot pistol clutched in one hand.

Hickok turned to thank the sergeant, but he and the other soldiers were gone, advancing toward the rebel line behind the rocky ledge, firing steadily.

Revolver in hand, Hickok hesitated.

There was fighting all around.

The horse was under control now, but Hickok could not remember which direction was west. He looked for the sun, but it had not yet cleared the tree line. There was now so much smoke drifting over the battlefield that it was difficult to see anything beyond a few dozen yards away. Then he heard the roar of a cannon, and, believing it to be the rebel battery again, he urged his horse in the opposite direction. But instead of crossing the creek once more, as he expected, he found himself at a rock fence. On the other side of the wall was a cornfield, and he could see men advancing cautiously through the stalks.

They were in uniform.

Relieved, he followed the wall until it came to an oak tree, then dismounted. He looped the reins around a low branch, then put his back against the tree and his boots against the rock fence. He waited, with a revolver in one hand.

Then there were gunshots in the cornfield, and a soldier vaulted over the rock fence and landed next to Hickok. He carried a big Enfield rifle, and his uniform was gray.

"It is a little fierce out there," the boy said in a Southern drawl, then pushed his cap back to the crown of his head. His blond hair was matted with sweat, and his face was smudged with gunpowder. "I lost my canteen in the first assault. Spare some water, cousin?"

Hickok nodded at the canteen slung over the horse's saddle.

"Thanks," the boy said. He left his rifle against the rocks and crawled over to the horse, uncapped the canteen, and took a long drink. He splashed some over his face, then smiled.

"You dry?"

Hickok hadn't realized how parched he had become. He took the canteen and took a long drink, then wiped his mouth with the back of his hand. He handed the canteen back to the boy.

"It has been a grand fight so far, don't you think?" the boy asked.

"It has been something," Hickok said.

"You hurt?" the boy asked.

"Not yet," Hickok said.

"You have a nice spot here," the boy said.

"It'll do for now," Hickok said.

"Hell, where are my manners?" the boy said, then held out his hand. "Jason Dupree, Third Louisiana Infantry."

Hickok shook his hand.

"You've come a long way for this," Hickok remarked.

"All the way from Pensacola," the boy said brightly.

"That's in Florida."

"Don't I know it? My daddy is friends with Colonel Hebert—that's our commander, damn him—and Daddy was mighty afraid the fighting would be over before I could kill me some Yankees. Since the revolution, all of us Dupree men have been army heroes. Daddy says this war will be over in a month, but my daddy is a fool. You from here?"

"Near enough," Hickok said.

"Thought so," he said. "You don't look like a soldier."

"You do," Hickok said.

"We do have some dashing uniforms, I reckon," the boy said. "Kind of hot, though. What time do you think it is now? I was always bad at judging time."

"Eight o'clock," Hickok said. "Maybe half past."

The boy nodded.

The fighting in the cornfield became fiercer.

"Sounds like somebody's taking a licking out there," the boy said. "But I can't tell which side. I think I'll just bide my time here for a spell."

"Good thinking," Hickok said.

"You scared?"

"Yes," Hickok said.

"Me, too," the boy said. "It ain't like I thought it would be. I figured that out right fast, after I saw one of them Yankees holding his guts in with one hand and crying for his mother. Then a fellow I marched all the way from Louisiana with got hit in the face and didn't have any face no more. That's all I wanted of being a hero. They don't tell you about all the blood in the storybooks, do they?"

"No, they don't," Hickok said.

"I reckon the first part of coming back a hero is staying alive long enough to come back," the boy said. "So my plan is to keep my head low and my butt lower."

"How old are you, son?"

"How old are *you*?"

"Twenty-five."

"You look older," the boy said.

"I feel older," Hickok said. "What are you, eighteen?"

"Seventeen."

"You're a cheerful child."

"That's because I believe I will live through this," he said. "Older folks, they start worrying about dying, and the scare makes them stupid. You worry about dying?"

"No," Hickok said. "I worry about living."

"You are a peculiar fellow," the boy said. "But I reckon you're all right. Anybody who is not shooting at me is all right by me."

"Ever think about going out west?" Hickok asked. "You have the disposition for it."

"Think so?"

"I know so," Hickok said.

"West, huh?" the boy asked. "Now, there's a notion. That would give my daddy fits."

There was a lull in the shooting. The boy took up his rifle and straightened his cap.

"Think it's over?"

"I don't know," Hickok said.

"Well, I reckon it's a good time to say farewell," he said. "Thanks for the water, mister."

Then he was over the fence.

Hickok looked at the sky. He could see the sun now through the trees, and it was in the opposite side of the sky from where he thought it should have been. But the fighting was still so fierce to the west that he mounted his horse and rode due east across the cornfield. He rode past dozens of bodies among the stalks, and when he crossed the creek it was red with blood.

As he was riding up a steep hillside, in the direction of the Wire Road, he met a rebel coming down. The man wore a homespun uniform, he carried an ancient shotgun in his hands, and he was half running and half sliding down the hill.

Twenty yards away, the rebel grabbed a sapling and slid to a stop. As the man brought up his shotgun, Hickok drew his revolver, but before he could fire, a shot came from the crest of the hill. The rebel fell, and he and the shotgun slid impotently down the hill.

Three Union soldiers stood atop the hill, one of them with a smoking rifle in his hand. Then there was a volley of rifle fire from beyond the hill, and two of the Union soldiers fell. The third took off running down the hill, tripped, and landed on the ground, frantically attempting to reload his rifle. A shot rang out and he fell, ramrod in his hand and a powder cartridge clutched in his front teeth.

Hickok fired two quick shots toward the rebels now clustered on the hilltop, then spurred his horse and made for the safety of a limestone bluff. An artillery battery opened up from across the creek bottom, and Hickok watched in horror as one of the shells struck the ground in front of his horse. It bounced lazily upward, like a stone skipped on a pond, and exploded in the trees far behind him. Then another shell struck near the hilltop, killing two of the rebels and scattering the rest.

Hickok reined his horse to a stop beneath the limestone bluff as two more shells tore apart the hillside above, showering him with bits of wood and dirt. Then an unarmed Union soldier dropped down from the bluff, his eyes wild, and he ran toward Hickok and tried to pull him from the saddle.

The horse reared, and Hickok and the soldier fell heavily to the ground. The riderless horse moved a few yards away, trailing the reins, and the soldier scrambled after it. Hickok lunged for the soldier and caught him by the legs, taking him down.

"Stop it," Hickok said.

"Let go of me, damn you," the man said, then struck Hickok in the nose with his fist.

"Like hell I will," Hickok said.

The soldier was out of breath. He was older than Hickok by a few years, shorter but heavier, and his blue eyes rolled wildly about.

Sitting on top of the man, Hickok drew a hand across his own face. It came away wet with blood.

"If you broke my nose," Hickok said, "I'll bust your head."

The soldier pulled a knife from his belt and swung. As Hickok reared back, the tip of the knife grazed his throat.

Hickok rolled off the man and came up holding a revolver.

The man scrambled backward, the knife still in his hand.

"Stay away from that horse," Hickok said.

The man was reaching behind him for the reins.

Hickok pulled the hammer back.

The man found the reins.

Before the soldier could get to his feet, Hickok fired. The .36-caliber ball struck the soldier in the chin and took away most of his lower jaw. The reins slipped from his hands, but instead of falling back he struggled to his feet, blood pouring onto his chest, and he staggered toward Hickok, the knife raised.

Still on the ground, Hickok cocked the revolver again. But before he could fire, a figure in homespun rushed by him and clubbed the bloody soldier in what was left of his face with the butt of a Sharps carbine. As blood flew in an arc toward the sky, the gruesome soldier spun and then crumpled to the ground, facedown.

The rebel soldier pulled a bowie knife, knelt on the fallen man's back, and drove the blade deeply into the right kidney, then twisted it. The soldier jerked, then lay still.

The rebel withdrew the knife and wiped the eighteen-inch blade on the soldier's woolen blouse.

"Ha!" he said. "That jawless sonuvabitch was quite a sight, coming at you with that little knife in his hand. Guess he wanted your horse something fierce."

"It would seem," Hickok managed. His own voice sounded alien, and he could feel his face swelling.

"Let me take a look at that," the rebel said, approaching Hickok. He was thin, and had long red hair and a beard to match, and from his speech Hickok knew he was a Texan. "Put that damned Colt down, before you shoot me."

The man placed the bony fingers of his right hand beneath Hickok's jaw, then lifted his head a bit and turned it to the right. Then he probed Hickok's nose with his thumb.

"Damn," Hickok said, and jerked away.

"I'll bet it smarts," the Texan said. "But I don't think it's broke. You're in a hell of a lot better shape than the Yank, poor devil. I almost feel sorry for him. I know you had the drop, but it seemed a waste of powder and ball to kill such a wretched creature with a pistol. Besides, I wasn't sure you would've pulled the trigger."

"I would have."

"But maybe only after that patch knife was in your windpipe." The Texan laughed. "I'm with the south Kansas–Texas cavalry, but I'll be damned if I know where they are since I got my horse shot out from under me. I was trying to make it to the rear, but looks like I wound up in the wrong spot. The fighting is so thick, it's like trying to outguess a wildfire. The worst of it is over on that hill yonder, which they tell me is called Oak Hill. That's where

Lyon has made his stand. Reckon they're going to call it Bloody Hill after this."

"What about Sigel?"

"The Dutch!" Bass said. "The fools came down the Wire Road toward the farmhouse, and old Ben McCulloch kicked the living shit out of them. They are hightailing it back to St. Louis by now, I reckon."

Hickok shook his head.

"Say, friend," Bass said. "Where do you call home?"

"Arkansas," Hickok said.

"Carroll's Cavalry, then," the Texan said as he returned the bowie knife to the scabbard he wore on his back. In front, tucked in his belt, was a big Walker Colt. "Cap'n Charles or Colonel DeRosey?"

"Charles," Hickok said.

"Huh, Charles Carroll only has forty men," the man said. "Thought I knew them all, but guess not. My name is Jedediah Bass, and I'm from all over Texas, but mostly my family hails from Bell County. You can call me Jed, if you've a mind."

Bass plucked Hickok's hat from the ground and offered it to him.

"Thanks," Hickok said, shaking dust from the black slouch hat. "I'm Jim. My people are from Yell County."

"You don't sound like you're from Arkansas."

"I grew up with an aunt in Illinois after my mother died birthing me," Hickok said, surprised at how easily the lie rolled from his tongue. "I came back to help Pa work the farm when I was eighteen, but I'm afraid I couldn't shake Illinois from my tongue."

"So, your family's divided?"

"I have an uncle with Fremont in St. Louis."

"Sad thing," Bass said. "But not an uncommon story. This your first scrap?"

Hickok nodded.

"I thought so," he said. "You have that lost look about you. It's a little different than shooting squirrels, ain't it? But don't worry. Your first fight is the worst."

"You don't look old enough to have been in others."

"Indians," Bass said. "Mexican bandits. I was a ranger before I joined up with old Ben McCulloch, damn him. He is one peculiar piece of humanity, a regular Old Testament patriarch who walks the earth and believes his commands come directly from the Almighty."

Hickok smiled.

Bass reached inside his shirt and scratched fiercely.

"I don't know what is worse, the pesky Yankees or these damned red bugs," he said. "This place is lousy with them, and they kept me awake most of last night."

Bass held out his hand and pulled Hickok to his feet. Blood was still rushing from his nose.

"You're bleeding like a stuck hog," Bass said.

Hickok pulled his handkerchief from his back pocket and held it tightly to his upper lip.

"Reckon we'd better fetch that hoss. Lord, is it hot already. It will be hot enough to fry eggs before noon." Bass removed his jacket, placed it on the ground, and laid his Sharps rifle on top of it.

"He's spooked," Hickok said through the cloth.

"Aw, he's a good animal. I can tell."

Bass made a low whistling sound and approached the horse, which backed away nervously.

"Come on, hoss," Bass said in a gentle voice. "I ain't gonna hurt you."

The horse shuffled its feet.

Bass placed a hand reassuringly against the left side of the animal's neck, then grasped the bridle with the other. The horse shook its head.

"Now, now," Bass said. "None of that."

With the animal still, Bass put a boot in a stirrup and swung into the saddle. He walked the horse in a circle, then removed his straw hat and gave Hickok a broad smile.

A line of rebels began descending the hillside above them.

"Come on, boys!" Bass shouted. "You'd better hurry up, because we're running out of Yankees!"

When the hundred or so rebels reached the bottom of the hill, an unseen Union battery began firing. Three rounds opened up craters in the ranks of the soldiers, and a fourth landed ten yards from Bass.

Horse and rider were thrown forward by a blossom of flame and smoke. The horse came down on its side, its feet tangled in its own intestines. Bass was trapped beneath, his foot still in the stirrup. A piece of the shell had pierced his side.

Hickok ran to him.

"Lord," Bass said through lips that were already flecked with bright red blood. "I think I should have let you fetch your own hoss. Damn, I figured the odds were against having another one go down with me."

The horse writhed in agony, and Bass grimaced.

"How bad am I hurt?"

Hickok hesitated.

"Tell me."

"You're lung-shot," Hickok said.

Bass closed his eyes.

Another shell hit seventy-five yards away, and Hickok could feel the ground shake and hear the shrapnel cut the air above their heads.

"We've got to get out of here."

Hickok grasped the man beneath the arms and pulled.

Bass screamed.

"No," he said. "I ain't going anywhere. There's half a ton of busted hoss on that leg."

The horse lifted its head and uttered a pitiful cry.

"A favor," Bass said, and took the big revolver from his belt. "Put him down quick, for he won't last. Use the Walker, because his skull is pretty thick."

Hickok took the gun, knelt in front of the horse, and placed the muzzle between the horse's eyes. Then he pulled the trigger and the animal lay still. He went back to Bass and tried to place the revolver back in Bass's hand, but the Texan pushed it away.

"One more favor," Bass said. "Me now."

"No," Hickok said.

"Please," he said.

"People heal," Hickok said.

"Not when they've been torn open by a jagged piece of iron casing," he said, then coughed blood. "And even if I could survive, I don't want to be a one-legged cripple. Don't argue, because I can't talk much longer. Don't let me bleed to death beneath a dead horse. If I don't pass out, then I'll be crying and screaming for water and begging for somebody to kill me. Don't let me beg."

Hickok nodded.

Bass managed a smile.

"Glad I met you, friend," he said. "It's good not to die alone. I've got a few things on my person I'd like returned to my family. Letters, mostly. Can you get them to McCulloch? He'll know how to get them back to Austin. My wife's there."

"What's her name?"

"Analuisa."

"I'll remember."

Hickok pulled the hammer back on the Walker.

"Funny, but I can't feel anything right now except those damned red bugs all over me."

"Close your eyes."

"No," Bass said. He was staring into the sky, his eyes following something. Hickok glanced up. A red-tailed hawk sailed high above the battlefield.

Hickok stood. He pointed the heavy revolver at the center of the Texan's chest, then pulled the trigger. The hammer fell on a dry chamber.

Bass managed a wry smile.

Hickok dropped the Walker and pulled one of his own Colt Navies. He cocked and fired, then fired again. Bass died with his eyes open.

Then Hickok dropped to his knees and hastily removed everything he could find from the dead man's vest pockets. There were letters, a small photograph in a leather case, and assorted papers. He stuffed these in his own pockets, then picked up the jacket and rifle from the ground and stumbled away.

Seventeen

The last place on earth Hickok wanted to be was Grand Prairie. He trudged among the dead and dying beneath the August sun, blood caked on his chin, his tongue growing thick in his mouth. He could not stand to look upon the bodies, where flies swarmed over gaping mouths and vacant eyes, and each breath brought with it the acrid sting of gunpowder and the stench of putrefaction. What an awful enterprise was war, he thought, and how unfortunate that he should find himself in the midst of it.

He paused in the middle of what had once been a cornfield—was it the same one lined by the rock fence, or another?—and could not help but stare at the body of a private. It was the boy with the wheat-colored hair who had challenged him just a few hours earlier. He lay on his back, his arms outstretched, as if nailed to a cross. The flattened stalks and leaves around him were stained dark with his blood. But the boy's face was serene, and in death he looked more like a sleeping girl than a soldier. In his right hand was clutched a small pasteboard, of the type handed out in Sunday school to students who knew their verses, depicting a contemplative Christ in the Garden of Gethsemane.

Jesus wept, Hickok thought.

Then the rattle of rifle fire and the booming of cannon forced him onward, past the cornfield and to the water of a branch east of Wilson Creek, and through a heavy thicket. He emerged from the thicket into an orchard of apple and peach trees, and from there spied a springhouse of arched stone. Confederate soldiers were clustered around the entrance, and there was a line of civilians, including some children, carrying buckets of water up the hillside to the Wire Road, and then across the road to a farmhouse with a broad porch at the summit of the hill.

Hickok walked over, cradled the carbine, and rested for a moment in the cool air at the mouth of the springhouse. A child struggled past him with a bucket, and he stopped her and plunged his hands into the cold water.

"You look awful bloody," the child, a girl of twelve or thirteen, said. "The rebels have turned the house into a hospital. A federal surgeon has stayed behind to help the wounded. Come along and I'll take you there."

Hickok drank from his cupped hands. He could not remember when water had tasted so good, and wondered why he had ever preferred whiskey.

"I'm not hurt in that way," Hickok told her.

He took the bucket from her and, holding it to his lips with both hands, drank until he could drink no more. Then he placed the bucket on the ground, dipped his kerchief into the water and washed his face, then repeated the operation twice more. When he was finished, the water had turned the color of wine.

"You look better now," she said.

She grabbed the rope handle and started to haul the bucket up the hill.

"No," Hickok said, taking the bucket from her. He tossed the contents on the ground, then returned the bucket and said, "It will be better if you get some fresh water for the wounded."

She nodded and disappeared into the depths of the springhouse. In a few moments she emerged, stains on her apron where her knees had pressed into the clay where she had knelt to scoop up more water.

Hickok smiled.

"Water is a wonderful thing."

"I like the springhouse," she said, clutching the bucket with both hands. "The water is so cold it makes your hands ache, even on the hottest days, and there are crawdads that live beneath the stones. No matter how many crawdads we catch, there are always more the next day. Where do you reckon they come from?"

"The earth," Hickok said. "Like all good things."

"They're fun to catch," she said. But then she frowned. "But snakes come from holes in the earth, too. I don't much care for snakes. I am powerfully afraid of stepping into a nest of copperheads. My daddy chops their heads off with a hoe."

"As well he should," Hickok said.

"I don't much like what's happening in the house," she said. "We hid in the basement along with our nigger for a spell, until the rebels took it over for their sick. The sounds coming from upstairs were too dreadful. So when Daddy said the fighting had shifted over to Oak Hill, I came outside to help."

"You're a good girl," Hickok said. "Run along now; the men need that water."

"Bye, stranger," she said, as matter-of-factly as if they had met outside a storefront in town, then walked on.

Hickok lingered in the cool of the springhouse, and he asked one of the men there about the progress of the battle.

"The Yankees are whipped," the man said, digging in his pockets for a twist of rough tobacco.

"But they killed about as many of us as we did of them, at least a thousand on each side." He found the tobacco, brought it out, and bit off a piece. Then he offered the twist to Hickok.

Hickok shook his head.

"Suit yourself," the man said, chewing. He turned his head and spit, then continued. "Most of them are in retreat. What's left is just a few skirmishers, trying to hold us off long enough to give them a head start. I reckon they will run all the way to Rolla, because by tonight Springfield is ours. Been there?"

"No," Hickok said.

"I'm damned tired of marching and sleeping on the ground," the man said. "The only thought in my mind is sleeping indoors tonight."

Hickok picked up the carbine and walked up the hillside, crossed the road, and continued up to the farmhouse. There were dozens of men and officers on the porch and in the yard, and litter bearers carrying wounded into the house from the beds of wagons and sometimes the tops of caissons. Hickok found a clear spot and looked across the creek bottom.

Turkey buzzards circled lazily in the morning sky.

Then there was a small commotion around a wagon on the road below, and a pair of orderlies walked a litter up the path to the house, in no hurry.

As they approached, a captain stepped down from the porch to examine their burden. The corpse was clad in a blue officer's uniform from the Mexican war.

"Where'd they find this one?"

"On the ground near that bloody hill," one of the orderlies said. "They just left him, apparently. We've shuffled him about a few times this morning, to try to get as many of the living up here as we could. But then we got orders from General Price to let the Yankee sawbones take a look at him."

The captain called for the surgeon, and word was relayed inside the house. Soon a tall man in a bloody apron appeared on the porch, wiping his hands with an equally bloody cloth.

"What is it, Captain?"

"Sir, do you know this man?"

The surgeon stepped over and gazed at the body. He reached out and touched the man's jacket, then reached up to touch his matted hair.

"It's Nathaniel Lyon," he said. "He's been shot at an angle through the breast, as if in the act of holding the bridle rein of his mount in his left hand and turning to shout words of encouragement to his troops."

"Dr. Melcher," the captain said, "you can tell all that just by looking at him?"

"Tell me, then, how else a general should die," the surgeon said. "Bring him into the house, if you please, and place him upon Mrs. Ray's bed, in the back."

After the orderlies had carried the body into the house and the doctor had followed, the captain folded his arms and looked out across the battle-field, watching the circling birds.

Then he glanced over at Hickok and frowned.

"You there," he called. "What's your name?"

"Bass," Hickok said.

"What's your story?"

"My horse was shot out from under me and I got separated from the rest of the men," Hickok said. "Came here for some water."

"Well, William, don't skulk around here like some goddamned spy," the captain said. "Use the legs God gave you and go find your unit."

Eighteen

Hickok did not know when he reached Arkansas. He had left the Wire Road around Dug Springs and cut to the southeast, walking through rolling hills in the morning and late in the afternoon, but resting through the heat of midday. More than a few of the farms he came to were deserted, the war having driven the owners away, and he slept in the barns and scavenged what he could from the cabins.

He took whatever small game came within range of his revolvers, and when he was near a creek or a river he would fish, using a line and some rusty hooks found on a dusty shelf in one of the cabins. He became even thinner, and his hair and beard grew wild, and he longed for someone to talk to. But as he went farther and the terrain grew steeper, any inhabitants he chanced upon kept him at such a distance that conversation was impossible. Once he met what appeared to be a father and two sons cutting timber along a rocky stream in an idyllic wood, and his cheerful hello was met with hostility. The men spoke not a word but held their axes at the ready until he moved on. Women and children were just as inhospitable, going inside their shacks and shutting the doors and watching with suspicion from behind tattered window curtains as he passed. It was a region where poverty and mistrust ruled, where neither telegraph nor railway had yet penetrated, and where the war had made the grim struggle for survival even more desperate.

Hickok cursed himself for losing the horse Lorenzo had given him, for the lack of planning and curiosity that had led him to wander across the battlefield at Wilson Creek, and for failing to memorize when he had the chance the course of streams and trails across the Ozarks. Even on the plains, he had always been in the company of others, even when he kept to himself, but now his solitude was complete. He longed for something to read, a book or a newspaper, and he wished he had the fiddle he had played often, but never well, in Kansas. He tried to remember the stories he had read in his youth, and to reconstruct them in his memory, but failed. He tried whistling, and then singing, but after he'd repeated the dozen or so tunes he knew well, the sound of his own noise gave him no comfort.

Then early one morning he followed a stream down to where a road crossed at a rock ford. Wagon ruts furrowed the bright orange earth of the road, which snaked away to the north and the south over the hills, and Hickok stood for a long while in the center of the road, thinking.

"There must still be some traffic on this meager artery," he said, for he had fallen at last into the habit of talking to himself. "By and by a rider or a wagon must pass, and then I will engage the travelers in some little conversation. Perhaps they will stop for water, for the stream here is sweet. Then my loneliness will be ended for a time, and perhaps even I may glean some bit of intelligence that will reveal my location in these rough hills."

Hickok found a spot on some rocks near the water, in the shade of the trees, placed his rifle on the ground so as not to appear too threatening, and buttoned his coat over the revolvers in his belt. Then he sat down on a large flat rock, adjusted his hat to block the fury of the sun, and proceeded to wait.

About noon, judging by the sun, he was rewarded by the sound of horses and the sharp sound of iron rims on stone from the north. Soon a coach pulled by a team of horses came into view, and the horses were doing little more than a walk. The coach was red with yellow wheels, and lashed to its top was a pine coffin. There were no passengers inside. As it neared the ford, it slowed. When the hooves of the horses splashed in the water, they began to drink, and the driver kicked down the brake.

Hickok gave a casual wave.

"You alone?" the driver called. He was a big man, of middle age and with a thick red beard, and he held the reins in one gloved hand and a double-barreled shotgun in the other.

"Yes," Hickok said.

"No companions waiting in the brush?"

"I am quite alone and wish you no harm," Hickok said. "I've been walking for days now and felt only joy at the sight of another."

The driver laughed.

"Joy, is it?" he asked. "Well, I've been the cause of much fear in other men, but you're the first that has confessed to such tenderness."

"The only living man I confess tender feelings for is my brother," Hickok said. "I allow warmth for my friends and an ember of hope for strangers."

"Well, fetch your skinny little ember over here," the man said. "I can't let these horses drink much longer or it'll twist their guts in this heat."

Hickok slowly picked up the carbine and rose.

"Uncap that thing."

Hickok took the percussion cap from the nipple and placed it in his pocket. Then he asked: "And what of these?"

He undid the button of his coat and swept it back to reveal the butts of the Navies.

"Hell, son, you're a walking arsenal."

"I think we are both well enough armed to inspire trust."

"Or dread."

"I lay down my arms for no man," Hickok said. "Continue on your way if it gives you pause. I will take no offense."

"Come on," the man said.

Hickok waded into the shallow water and climbed onto the seat, placing the carbine beside him. The driver released the brake and urged the team on.

"Deserter?"

"No," Hickok said. "I search for my brother. When last my family received word, he was somewhere in Arkansas with the Texas cavalry. We fear the worst."

"You a soldier?"

"I was a ranger," Hickok said. "Once I find my brother, I aim to join him—or to take his place if he is dead."

"Where's your horse?"

"Shot from beneath me when I encountered a band of cutthroats below Fort Smith," he said. "I am ashamed to say that I made only one of them pay for their crime."

"You're charmed," he said. "Murderers and thieves are as thick as crows in these parts. The

Butterfield line stopped running at the outbreak of the war, and now they're threatening to stop even the local coach runs."

"And your grim cargo?"

"Oh, the deader," the driver said. "This is a special run to bring the husk back to Yellville for burial. Her name was Tutt and she died up in Forsyth a day ago. She paid in advance to be brought back to the family plot, war or none. It pays handsomely, and it is the first time I've never had a passenger complain about the ride. You might as well travel all the way with me, because Yellville would be a good place to look for your lost brother. There have been a lot of soldiers passing through this summer. When's the last time you ate?"

"Yesterday," Hickok said. "Shot a rabbit."

"Well, there's some vittles under the box," the driver said. "Ain't much, just some apples and corn bread, but you're welcome to it."

"I'm obliged," Hickok said.

"You might want to clean up some when we get to Yellville, if you have any spending money," the driver said. "You look wild enough to scare the dead."

"She doesn't seem to mind," Hickok said. "So, toward which side of this fight do you lean, if you don't mind me asking?"

"I'm for whichever side is winning," the driver said. "Today, I'm whistling 'Dixie.' Tomorrow, I might be humming a different tune. I don't reckon it matters none, because the Ozarks is a savage little nation all by itself."

Nineteen

The coach kept rolling through the rest of the afternoon and into the night. When the new moon rose in the east, Hickok realized it had been a full month since the battle. He shifted his long frame on the rough seat and tried to sleep, but the road was too rough to permit it. Finally he gave up and asked the driver what he knew of Yellville.

"Not enough to put in a teacup," he said. "I've been there often enough, when the coach was running regular, but folks there are a clannish and hot-tempered lot."

Shortly after midnight they pulled to a stop in the middle of a dark wood, and the driver broke out some feed for the horses and allowed them to eat and rest. There were no stations along the road any longer, he said, and it was too risky to unhitch the team. The horses would have to rest in harness.

Then he threw Hickok a blanket and told him to get some sleep, as they would be pulling out again before daybreak.

"Aren't you going to rest?"

"Not in these woods," the driver said.

"Then I will spell you in a couple of hours," Hickok said. He took the blanket and crawled into the coach, where he made himself comfortable by reclining on one bench and propping his boots on the other. He soon fell into a dreamless sleep.

He woke to the sound of a gun clattering to the ground.

"Hand down your gold, you red-bearded old fool. We know you have a chest beneath that seat, and we aim to have it."

Hickok peered out and saw three men on horseback, their faces covered by flour sacks with ragged holes cut out for the eyes. Two of them held rifles, and the third—the one doing the talking—had a revolver in one hand and a torch in the other.

The driver's shotgun was on the road.

"I told you, there ain't no gold on this trip," the driver called. "This is a special delivery. The only thing I'm haulin' is that box you see on top."

"We'll have to see what's inside that box."

"Can't you morons see that it's a coffin? What do you suppose you'll find inside?"

"We'll have a look-see all the same," the third man said, and he motioned for the smaller of the men to check it out. He handed his rifle over to the other one, and dismounted.

Hickock ducked low onto the floor of the coach as the man approached. The springs groaned as he climbed up over the boot to the top.

"It's nailed shut."

"Of course it is." The driver snorted.

Hickok heard the sound of a knife cutting rope, and then there were some scraping sounds as the man edged the coffin over the rails. The coffin fell to the ground, and Hickok heard the crack of wood.

The man on the coach jumped down.

"Good Lord, there is a powerful smell," he said.

"Can you see inside?"

"It's busted a bit, but the lid's still on tight."

"Make sure. Open it."

"I don't know, Chance," the man on the ground said. "I think there is a corpse in there, and I don't feel right about disturbing the dead."

The man with the torch began to cuss.

"You superstitious, mule-brained sonuvabitch," he said. "Don't you think they could have filled it with dead cats or something to throw us off the track of the gold? Open the damned lid and make sure."

"If it were filled with gold, it would be too heavy to lash to the top of the coach," the man protested. "You look, because I ain't touching it."

"Lord, save me from men with the minds of children," the man with the torch said as he placed the revolver in his belt and swung down from his horse. "It doesn't have to be gold; it could be anything," he said as he gave the torch to the other man. "Paper money don't weigh much." The makeshift mask was hampering his vision, so he lifted the front and tucked it up on the top of his head. Then he drew a knife, knelt beside the coffin, and drove the blade beneath the lid and pried.

The nails screamed as he forced the lid up.

"Don't do that, Chance," the man on the ground said, backing away. "It makes my skin crawl."

"Shut up."

He applied pressure, producing the noise again.

The lid was now up a few inches, and he reached down and grasped it with both hands and pulled. The lid came off, hinges and all, and the man beckoned for the torch.

The other man threw it to him.

He caught it, then held the torch low over the coffin.

Inside was the body of an old woman, resting on straw.

"Satisfied?" the driver asked.

"Old bitch," the man said, and kicked the coffin.

"Don't do that, Chance," the other man on the ground pleaded.

"Let's get out of here," the man on horseback said.

"We ain't leaving empty-handed," the one

called Chance said. "You sure you don't have anything worth our trouble inside the coach?"

"Nothing you'd want," the driver said.

"I'll be the judge," he said, and jerked open the
door to the coach. In the light of the torch, he saw
Hickok on the floor, with both Navies drawn.

He dropped the torch and went for his gun, but
his hand had barely touched the butt when Hickok
fired both of his revolvers. The balls struck him
squarely in the chest, and the force pushed him
back over the coffin and onto the road, face-first.

The driver snatched up the Sharps from below
the dashboard, where it had gone unseen, and
leveled it at the mounted robber. He pulled the
trigger, but the hammer fell impotently on the uncapped nipple.

The rider holding the two rifles across his saddle brought one up and shot the driver in the
chest.

As Hickok came out of the coach, the man on
the ground ran and snatched up the shotgun. He
had thumbed both hammers back when Hickok
shot him in the stomach. He stumbled backward,
discharging one of the barrels of the shotgun into
the ground, but did not drop the weapon.

Hickok recocked the revolver in his right hand
and put a ball into the man's shoulder. As he went
down, he lost his grip on the shotgun, and it struck
the ground butt first—and discharged its load of

buckshot upward into the side of the man's face, nearly decapitating him.

The team shuffled nervously and took a few steps forward. The brake had been set on the coach, and the wheels slid in the dirt a few feet before the team stopped.

Then Hickok turned to the man on horseback, who had dropped the gun he had shot the driver with and was bringing up the other. Hickok fired twice, once with each gun. One ball missed, but the other caught his left shoulder as he aimed the rifle. He dropped the weapon and wheeled his horse, and was soon out of the circle of light thrown by the torch on the ground. Hickok fired twice more at the sound of the retreating hooves, but had no hope of finding his mark in the darkness.

Hickok ran to the front of the coach. The driver was dead, slumped over in the seat, his hands dangling over the side to the ground.

He tucked his revolvers into his belt, picked up the torch from the road, and surveyed the carnage: two dead bandits, one dead driver, and the body of an old woman in a broken coffin upon the ground. Blood was everywhere, including on the corpse and coffin, and in the torchlight it shone a vibrant shade of red.

One of the bandits' horses had bolted and was gone, but the other had been well trained. It was standing a dozen yards away, head down, waiting.

By dawn Hickok had tied the lid back on the coffin and gotten it back on top of the coach, and had put the bodies of the dead bandits and the driver inside, along with the guns. He put a lead on the bandit horse and tied it to the back of the coach.

Then he climbed up into the seat and spread a blanket, so he wouldn't have to sit in the driver's blood, and took up the reins. As he released the brake and urged the team on, he reflected on what a macabre sight the coach and its passengers must present.

Twenty

It was raining when the coach rolled down the muddy and deserted street that ran through the center of town. Hickok pulled wearily on the reins, then pushed the brake down with his foot and looped reins over the handle. Water poured from the brim of his hat as he swung down from the seat and planted his boots in the mud.

A boy in his early teens emerged from the shadows of one of the porches, his eyes glued to the coffin atop the coach. The boy wore little more than rags, his face was smudged with dirt, and his wild straw hat drooped in the rain. He ambled toward Hickok on bare feet, mud oozing between his toes.

"Hey, there," the boy said.

"Hey, yourself," Hickok said. "Where is everybody?"

"Sunday morning," he said. "They're all in

church, asking forgiveness for the things they done with each other on Saturday night."

"I take it you're not a praying man."

The boy smiled.

"Never acquired the habit," he said. "Besides, my natural talent is for sin."

Hickok laughed.

"Who's in the box?"

"An old woman by the name of Tutt."

"And these fellers?" the boy asked. He had climbed up and was looking inside the door of the coach.

"Get down from there," Hickok said. "And I don't know their names."

"They are a powerful wicked sight," the boy said, then whistled before he jumped back down to the mud. "How'd they come to such a bloody end?"

"They tried to rob us on the road."

"Us?"

"The one with the red beard was the driver of this coach. They killed him."

"And you killed the other two?"

"Yes," Hickok said.

The boy whistled again.

"Mister, you are the original angel of death," he said, "with hell in both hands. Those revolvers, they are Colt's Navies, aren't they? Civilian models, I reckon, what with the brass straps."

"How you do go on."

"Oh, I know my guns," the boy said proudly.

"You'd do better to study your arithmetic."

"Damn, mister, I don't go to school."

"Watch your language," Hickok said. "You know how to read?"

"I can write my own damned name well enough."

Hickok gave him a stern glance.

"It's hard not to cuss," the boy protested.

"Try," Hickok suggested. "You recognize any of the dead?"

"Nope."

"Know anybody named Tutt?"

"Tons. Let me have a look," the boy said, then began climbing up into the seat of the wagon and was almost to the coffin when Hickok caught him by the seat of the pants and hauled him back down.

"No," he said. "What I meant was, can you fetch somebody named Tutt to come claim the body?"

"Maybe I can and maybe I can't," the boy said.

"I don't have any money," Hickok said.

"Oh, I don't want no money," the boy said. "My pa would just beat me until I coughed it up, anyway. No, sir, what I want is to be your friend."

"My friend?"

"Yes, sir," the boy said.

"Why?"

"I'd like you to meet my pa," the boy said.

"You want me to whip your father?"

"Not necessarily," the boy said. "I just want him to know that you could."

"Perhaps he's bigger than I am."

"He's not."

"Perhaps he's meaner than I am."

"Not likely," the boy said. "The only person he thumps on is me, and then only when he's drunk."

"What's your name, boy?"

"Jackson. What's yours?"

"William Bass," Hickok said. "But my friends call me Wild Bill. You can be my friend if you try not to cuss and promise to judge men by the quality of their actions and not the guns they wear."

They shook.

"Pleased to make your acquaintance, Wild Bill."

"It's time to fetch those Tutt relations you say you know."

"Sure thing," the boy said. He turned to the row of drab buildings, cupped his hands around his mouth, and yelled, "You there, Mister Tutt! Get your sorry—"

Hickok grasped his shoulder.

"Go quietly and bring him here," Hickok said. "And don't blurt out everything you know. This woman was a family member, and you will show some respect."

Jackson nodded, then slipped from Hickok's grasp and ran up on the porch of a building. A rough sign out front proclaimed it was the White

River Tavern. The boy looked in the window, then slipped inside the door.

A few moments later a man in his middle twenties walked outside, pulling on a long leather coat. He was of average height, but powerfully built, and he had a full head of sand-colored hair and a short beard to match. He held a cigar between his teeth, and his green eyes narrowed against the smoke as he leisurely donned a wide-brimmed hat sporting a turkey feather in the band.

Jackson stood behind him anxiously.

"You have business with me?" the man called from the porch.

"Your name Tutt? Then I have business."

The man took in Hickok and the coach and the coffin on top, and his green eyes flickered while Hickok explained that it had fallen on him to deliver the body.

"I don't know who she is, other than her last name is Tutt," Hickok said. "The driver told me she fell ill and paid him in advance to bring her here from Taney County in Missouri. Have you not received word?"

"None," Tutt said.

He walked slowly toward Hickok, moving as if pulled reluctantly by the shoulders. When he was a few steps away from Hickok he turned, hiding his face.

"My mother stayed behind in Taney County a few weeks ago to put things in order after she had buried a cousin who had died of the fever," he said. Tears ran down his cheeks. "I was to retrieve her in a fortnight."

"I'm sorry," Hickok said.

Tutt's body remained still, but his eyes were wild.

"Perhaps it's not her," he said.

"The odds of that seem slim," Hickok said.

Tutt moved toward the coach, but Hickok grasped his arm.

"You don't want to do that," he said. "She has been dead for some days, it has been a rough trip, and she needs some attention before being viewed by a son."

Tutt pulled away from Hickok.

"There's been some mistake."

"I think not."

"You have seen the body?"

"An older woman, perhaps sixty, with long gray hair—"

"Oh, God!"

"—and a wedding band on her right hand."

Tutt fell to his knees and drove his fists into the mud. Then he lifted his face to the sky and screamed like a wounded animal.

"Mother!" he screamed. "Why did I let you stay behind? I should have insisted that you come home with the rest of us. You gave me life and I have thrown away yours!"

"Come now," Hickok said, and placed a hand on his shoulder.

Tutt knocked it away.

"To hell with you," he said.

"Stop it. Now."

Tutt reached up and grasped the lapels of Hickok's coat.

"You don't understand," he said. "I killed her as surely as if I had burst a cap against her skull. My mother was the world to me—my mother was the rock upon which my life was built, the harbor that sheltered me from the raging storm, the person who carried my burdens as her own. What shall I do without her?"

"Live, I reckon."

"You are a heartless sonuvabitch," Tutt said. "Have you no mother of your own? Do you care so little for your own sweet mother? Do you not share the bond that not even death can break—"

"Please."

Tutt threw himself backward in the mud and tore open his shirtfront, exposing his chest to the rain. Then he began to roll in the mud, and Jackson stepped forward and snatched up his hat before it was flattened.

"Get up," Hickok urged.

Tutt raked his fingernails across his own cheeks and then grasped his hair with both hands and began to tear out tufts.

"Stop it. Damn, boy, what do you know of this man?"

"His blood runs hot," the boy said.

Tutt wailed, rolled again, then drew up on one knee. He was covered in mud, his face was bleeding, and he moaned pitifully. Then his hand drew the big Remington revolver from his belt and cocked it while bringing the barrel beneath his chin.

"No," Hickok said as he reached for the revolver.

The hammer fell and pinched the flesh between Hickok's thumb and forefinger, and he let out a howl as he drew the revolver away and tossed it into the mud. Tutt lunged after the weapon, but the boy snatched it up before he could reach it. Then Hickok fell on top of the man, trying to pin his arms, but Tutt was too strong for him. Soon Tutt was on top of him, trying to snatch the Colt's from his waist.

"Jackson!" Hickok shouted.

The boy stepped forward and expertly rapped the butt of the Remington against the back of Tutt's head. Tutt stiffened, then fell unconscious into the mud.

"Where in hell did you learn that?" Hickok asked.

"I work in the saloon, cleaning up after the drunks," the boy said. "I've seen old Davis here do it a hundred times to others. I don't reckon you can do that with arithmetic, can you, Wild Bill?"

"Reckon not," Hickok said as he removed the belt from Tutt's coat and tied his hands with it. "Boy, you did the right thing. I was afraid I was going to have to shoot the silly bastard to keep him from killing himself."

"What would have been the point in that?"

"Exactly," Hickok said.

"That was some fight," the boy said with enthusiasm. "I've never seen anybody get the best of Davis here, but you gave him a run for his money. I'll bet you could have taken him, if you hadn't been trying to help him instead."

"Don't believe it," Hickok said, wincing from what felt like a hundred bruises. "I could not have won with my fists. If we ever squared off for real, I would have to shoot him."

"Aw, that ain't going to happen. You saved his life."

"No," Hickok said. "You did that."

"Better not tell how I whacked him," the boy said. "It would hurt his pride something fierce, and you can see what happens when old Davis is feeling down on himself. Let's just keep it between friends."

Hickok nodded.

"Son, I need you to run down to that church where you say all the decent and hypocritical folks are and bring back three—no, four—of the biggest men to watch after Mister Davis Tutt for a spell."

"Splendid notion," the boy said. He switched

the Remington from hand to hand, then pointed it at the saloon sign. "Forty-five caliber. Kicks like a rifle, and leaves a hole just as big."

"Explain about the passengers in the coach. Ask the men with the strongest stomachs to help me take care of the mess in the coach, but don't let them bring any of their women with them. Understand?"

"Count on me," the boy said. "Do you want me to go to the other church and tell Mister Davis's brother?"

"Didn't know he had a brother," Hickok said. "But yes, he should know their mother is dead as well—unless he shares Davis Tutt's talent for madness."

Jackson laughed. He tucked the Remington beneath the rope that held up his trousers.

"Why, Lewis is as sound as the North Star. They have different mothers—but you'll see for yourself."

"When you get back, please be certain the men get that team unhitched and taken to the livery and cared for. Guess that would be the place for the coach as well, until the owner can come claim the lot."

"What about the animal behind the coach?"

"That's my horse now," Hickok said. "Think you can take care of him personally?"

"Why, I allow I can," the boy said enthusiastically. "I know the smith—hell, I know everybody in town—and I will make him understand the situation."

"Well, tell said blacksmith that I will brook no stealing from the dead," Hickok said. "Whatever they have on their persons is to remain there. And that goes for you as well, since you've already told me where your talents lie."

"Why, Bill," Jackson said, feigning disappointment. "I never steal from friends."

"It's a start."

The boy turned to go.

"Jackson," Hickok called. "Leave that hog leg on the porch, where Davis Tutt can find it later, if you please."

After the boy had gone, Hickok walked over to the coach and swung up on the door. He looked over the bodies, then reached in and removed the flour sack from the head of one of the dead bandits.

Despite the bloodstains, Hickok could read the printing on the sack: WHITE RIVER MILL.

Twenty-one

It was afternoon by the time the team had been unhitched and the bodies taken from the coach, the blood washed from the interior with many buckets of water, and the coffin carried into the deserted saloon of Davis Tutt.

The rain had stopped, and Hickok stood alone in the middle of the street. He was filthy, his shoulders sagged with fatigue, and his boots felt as if they were filled with lead. It seemed his life were a series of lonesome moments linked by violence, and he wondered if there would ever be a time he could truly rest.

He trudged over to the saloon, mounted the wooden steps, and eased himself onto a bench on the porch. He was nearly asleep when a voice called gently, "Mr. Bass?"

Hickok opened his eyes.

Before him was a slim woman in her middle twenties. She had blond hair and blue eyes, a high forehead and a slim nose, and lips that were thin but not cruel.

Hickok began to rise.

"Please, no," she said. "You look spent."

"I look quite many things, I imagine," Hickok said, as he got to his feet. "But my mother would insist that I rise in the presence of . . . a lady." Hickok had almost used the word *angel*, but checked himself.

The woman smiled.

"Your rough looks belie your upbringing," she said. "Forgive me for disturbing you, but I would be grateful for your counsel."

"How can I help?"

"My name is Susannah Moore and I have long been a friend of the Tutt family, for better and worse," she said. "My father was their preacher, when they felt the need to attend. My father has been gone since last summer, so it falls to me to make the preparations for the funeral of the mother, which under the circumstances must take place as soon as possible. In the morning, in fact."

"That is wise," Hickok said. "How may I help you?"

"Davis Tutt and his brother, Lewis, would be glad for you to keep the deathwatch with them tonight."

"I would be glad as well," Hickok said, "but I

must decline because of my appearance. It would be a matter of some disrespect."

"Appearances are often deceptive," Susannah said. "But there are a bath and some suitable clothes for you upstairs, if you would do us the favor."

Hickok hesitated.

"Why does this task fall upon you?" he asked. "Is this Lewis Tutt as incapacitated by grief over the woman's death as poor Davis?"

"No," she said. "Davis and Lewis are half brothers. They share a father, but different mothers. The father died long ago, and the mother had her differences with Lewis, which leaves him in an awkward position. He is here, however, to offer a shoulder to his brother."

"It is good to have family."

"Yes, it is," Susannah said. "Lewis, who is of your build, has given the clothes. They are yours to keep, if you care to."

"I am not in the habit of taking charity."

"It is not charity," she said. "It is kindness."

"Then I am grateful."

"Good," she said, and smiled. "I must go to help the women with the linen shroud, which is required by the poor woman's dreadful appearance. The furniture maker is busy with a suitable coffin. It will be ready by morning."

Hickok nodded.

"How fares Davis Tutt?" he asked.

"A wreck," Susannah said. "But he has folks around him now, and I expect they will convince him to obey God's canon against self-slaughter."

"You know your Shakespeare."

She blushed.

"Davis Tutt is certainly the melancholy prince of Yellville," she said. Then she cocked her head and peered at Hickok's face. "And what of you, Mr. Bass? Where do you call home, if I may be so bold?"

"I am a stranger on the plain," Hickok said.

"So you know your music," she said.

"I'm afraid I don't catch your meaning."

"No matter," she said, then smiled again. "Well, I must not keep you, unless you desire to bathe in cold water. You may take the stairs alongside the house to the upper floor. You will be undisturbed. There are some shaving implements laid out for you as well. There is a bed, and please take a nap, if you can sleep in this heat, for the watch will last all night."

She paused.

"What is it, Miss Moore?"

"That waif Jackson has gone on so about you, I expected you to be ten feet tall." She lowered her head, but cast her eyes up toward his. "Now I see that you are only nine."

Twenty-two

Hickok struck a match and lit a coal-oil lamp on the table, adjusted the flame, and took down the cloth that had been draped over the mirror. He hardly knew the face that stared back at him from the glass. The bath had washed away the blood and grime, but he was unprepared for the thicket of beard and the sharpness of his features. Only his steel blue eyes seemed familiar.

He poured some water from a pitcher into the basin, whipped up some soap in a cup, lathered his face, and took up the straight razor. He lifted his chin and placed the blade against his neck, drew it upward—and yelped in pain.

"Damn," he muttered to himself.

"Mister Bass?"

He turned. Susannah Moore was in the doorway.

"I'm in my drawers here," he said, alarmed.

"I just wanted to make certain the clothes were acceptable," she said. "And you're not the first man I've seen in his underwear."

They exchanged an embarrassed look.

"No, it's nothing like that," she said. "I tended to my father for many years before he passed. I just wanted to make sure that the clothes were agreeable."

"They are fine," he said. "I prefer black."

"You slept?"

"Yes, thank you."

He lifted the razor awkwardly and turned to the mirror again, anxious to end the conversation.

"Would you take some help? I helped my father often, when he was in decline."

Before he could answer, she stepped over and took the razor from his hand.

"Sit down, please."

As he took a seat on the stool, she replaced the cloth over the mirror.

"Superstitious?" he asked.

"Not particularly," she said. "But it is our way. Don't you have similar funeral practices where you come from?"

She stood behind him, took his face in her hands, and tilted his head to one side. She began to shave his neck in swift, sure strokes.

"You didn't answer me," she said. "Where is it that you come from?"

"Texas," he said, immediately filled with guilt for the lie.

"You don't sound like you're from Texas."

He was acutely aware of her fragrance—it was a clean, warm smell, a mixture of honeysuckle and clothes hung on a line to dry in the spring.

"I grew up in Illinois," he said.

"Ah," she said. "That explains your speech. Were you raised on a farm?"

"Yes," he said. "My brother left for Texas some years before and has a family there. He joined with McCulloch and was here in Arkansas, at last word, and he was very sick."

"So he was not with McCulloch at Oak Hill?"

"No," he said. "At Springfield, they directed me south. At Dug Springs, they said he was too sick to travel and had been removed to a safer location to recover, but they could not tell me where. The stage driver—the dead one—told me that I had best look here, where there had been a concentration of troops lately."

"Captain Mitchell raised several companies of men last month, from many counties nearby," she said.

"How many men?"

"About a thousand men marched out of town to join the boys in Missouri," she said. "If your brother recovered, perhaps he is now with them. What's his name?"

"Jed." Another pang of guilt.

"Jed Bass. I will remember it," she said, rinsing the razor in the basin. "And you are Bill?"

"My name is James," he said.

"But Jackson said—"

"Wild Bill is a nickname," he said.

"Men and their nicknames," Susannah said. "You all are little boys just pretending to be grown-up, aren't you? All of these secret signs between you."

She paused, stepped back, and judged her progress.

"Now, James, what do you think—should you be clean-shaven, or do you prefer I leave the mustache? I think we should leave it."

"Yes," he said.

"But we must do away with the muttonchops."

She worked a little more with the razor, then picked up a pair of scissors.

"It's fine, I'm sure," he said. "You can stop."

"Not yet," she said.

"It makes me uncomfortable."

"Do you think my work is unflattering? Or have I nicked you?"

"It is not the blade I fear, as long as your hand wields it," he said. "It is simply that I am undeserving of such attention."

"Be still," she said, and continued. "Tell me, James, if you are from Illinois and your brother has thrown in with Texas, was there not considerable friction between the two of you?"

"My older brother has made the choice for us both," he said. "If I find that he has indeed fallen from his illness, then I will take his place."

"So there may be two dead brothers instead of one?"

Hickok did not answer.

"I did not mean to offend," she said, drying his face with a washcloth. "Forgive me, for the Bible makes a poor patriot of me."

"How so?"

"One of the commandments, as I recall, prohibits killing," she said.

She took up a brush and smoothed his hair.

"The women I know would give anything for hair like this," she said. "On most men I would say it is a waste, but not on you. It does need trimming, however."

"I prefer it long," he said. "It is the style on the plains."

"Don't worry; I won't take much," she said as she reached for the scissors again. "So, you were on the plains as well, betwixt here and Illinois."

"I was a scout," he said. "Worked for the Overland Company in the territories. Then came the war."

"I see," she said, snipping. "So do you leave anyone behind you, either in Illinois or the territories or wherever else you have been?"

"You are a mite forward."

"And you are evasive," Susannah said. "You will soon find, Mister Bass, that I embrace the truth with passion. I have lived here in Yellville for so long that I've forgotten there is a world beyond these hills. You, Mister Bass, are a hint of that world beyond—and you make me uncomfortable as well. You may be a thief, a liar, a bushwhacker—or a knight-errant. Which is it, Mister Bass?"

"The jury is still out."

"Another deflection," she said. "So, is there someone?"

"My mother," he said. "In Illinois."

"That is all?" she asked. "No wife or girlfriend or sweetheart?"

"Nor any combination," he said.

"Was there ever anyone?"

"Not that I care to discuss."

"As you wish," Susannah said. "But the look in your eyes speaks volumes."

She touched his hair lightly, then placed the brush and the scissors on the desk.

"I think we are done," she said. "My, but you clean up nicely. None will believe you are the same wild creature who rolled into town this morning."

"And what of you?" Hickok asked.

"What of me, Mister Bass?"

"Is there someone?"

"Davis Tutt had intentions toward me," she said, "but he is not the steadiest star in the sky. I am fond enough of him, of course, but he has devoted such serious study to sin that I cannot imagine sharing his life. I'm afraid I buried the only man I ever loved when my father died."

Twenty-three

Hickok stood for a moment just inside the door of the saloon, temporarily blinded by the rows of candles that surrounded the walnut coffin placed upon a long table in the center of the room. On the lid of the coffin was a wreath of red roses, and the table was trimmed with black drapes. The mirror over the bar was covered with the Arkansas state flag.

"Bass," Davis Tutt called from a corner, where he was surrounded by stern-faced men who seldom took their eyes from him.

Hickok walked slowly across the room, his hands feeling the edges of tables and the backs of chairs as he passed. Tutt rose as he approached, and grasped Hickok's right hand in both of his own.

"Mister Tutt," Hickok said.

"Call me Dave," he said. "I want you to meet my brother. Lewis, this is the man who refused to surrender the stagecoach to the bushwhackers and completed the mission of delivering Mother back home. Without him, her body would still be on the road between here and Taney County."

"So you're Bass," Lewis Tutt said as he rose from his chair. He waited for Hickok to offer his hand first, and when he did, Lewis Tutt smiled broadly.

"You're brothers," Hickok said. "Well, at least it will be easy enough to tell you apart."

"It does surprise most people," Lewis Tutt said. "I'm not a slave, if that's the question on your mind. I'm as free as you or Davis."

"All men are free at birth," Hickok said. "Or should be."

"That can be an unpopular sentiment in these parts."

"I've never cared a whit for what is popular, only for what is right," Hickok said. The men around them shifted uncomfortably.

"There are few slaves in Marion County, Mister Bass," one of them said. "Our sympathies lie with the protection of our homes and families from Yankee invaders."

"My sentiments are with you," Hickok said, then turned back to Lewis. "I am pleased to meet you, Mister Tutt, and many thanks for the fine clothes."

"The clothes suit you," he said. "And I'd be pleased if you called me Lewis."

"And you may call me Wild Bill, if you like."

"You are well named," Lewis said. "I have seen your handiwork in the stable. You must be quite good with those irons, as the two dead bushwhackers attest."

"There were three," he said. "I sent a ball into his shoulder before he fled. Do you have any idea who the dead are?"

"No," Lewis said. "These hills are thick with ruffians. They come from everywhere and nowhere. We searched their pockets, but turned up only trash."

"Sit down," Davis said, "and have a sip of whiskey."

He poured a glass half-full and shoved it across the table as Hickok drew up a chair.

"You seem to have recovered," Hickok said, then took a gulp from the glass. It was the strongest whiskey he had ever tasted, and his reaction must have been evident in his face.

"Ha!" Davis said. "You've never tasted White River lightning before. Go easy on it, or it will have you howling at the moon. Would you care for some branch water to cut it with?"

"I prefer it full-bore," he said.

"As I do," Davis said. "It is the only thing that is going to get me through this long night. My grief tears at my heart like a hungry bird."

"So let us fill the time with conversation," Hickok said. "Tell me of Yellville, and your family's story in it."

"That conversation," Davis said, "would last a week's worth of nights. But I will attempt to give you a brief account. Have you ever heard of the Tutt-Everett War?"

Hickok shook his head.

"Some fifteen years ago, our father, Hamp Tutt, came into opposition with the Everett clan, which occupied most of the offices in the county. Nobody remembers how the trouble started, except that the Everetts and the Tutts hated one another at first sight."

"It happens sometimes."

"Old Hamp ran a grocery out of this building, and the Everetts resented how popular he became. He was a gambler and loved all manner of fun. Perhaps the Everetts resented his easy association with people of a different hue, and his casual relationship to marriage. It wasn't long after he came here that he was supporting two families. Whatever else you can say about old Hamp, he took his responsibilities seriously, and never once did he treat Lewis differently than he treated me, even though some of the townsfolk had a rather unpleasant term for Lewis. Hamp always took vigorous exception to this. Just as easily as he made friends, he made enemies."

"Men who think for themselves often do,"

Hickok said. "Tell me, at what point does the Moore family enter this drama?"

"I see you are curious about Susannah," Davis said. "Most men are. Her father, the Reverend Moore, was a devout pacifist and did his best to keep the peace. He was also a bit touched in the head, as all Millerites are, and one October during this period of trouble he gave away all of his possessions and repaired to Bald Jess, the hillside where his church stands, and waited for the world to end. It didn't, but he kept the faith with his far-flung brothers, and in a flurry of letters with them came to believe that Miller himself had simply gotten the biblical math wrong. The next October he did it all again, waiting for dawn in the cold and dressed in nothing but a flowing white robe. When the world was intact at the end of the day of the Second Great Disappointment, he put those curious notions aside and decided to do good on earth instead. He took Lewis here under his wing, taught him to read and write, and gave him the moral instruction that I, sadly, have lacked."

"And what of Hamp?" Hickok said. "He must have been a man of considerable size and skill to survive such strife."

"Hamp was a rather small man, but he had a powerful number of friends in the county who came to his aid, even to the point of taking up arms on his behalf, and the war raged for many years,

with much bloodshed on both sides. The governor
even sent the militia to cool things down."

"How was it resolved?"

"There were many desperate fights, and a few
miracles. Once, when the two sides were facing off
in the street yonder, up came a whirlwind and
blew dust in their faces and took away their hats.
It scared both sides so much they gave up for a
time. But eventually our faction killed a couple of
the Everett brothers. Then another Everett came
from Texas to avenge his brothers. This Everett
was arrested and put into jail for a spell, but his
friends tore open the jail and freed him. Open war-
fare raged for a time, and by and by our father was
killed in an ambush. Then the Everett from Texas
fled down the White River in a canoe, took a
steamboat to Shreveport—and died there of the
cholera."

"And thus the Tutts have remained."

"Indeed we have," Davis said. "And what of
you, Bill? Does your father still live?"

"He died when I was young."

"Then we four—Lewis and I, you and Susannah—
we are a band of orphans, are we not?"

"At least where our fathers are concerned."

Hickok took another drink. A familiar warmth
was coursing through his body, and he suddenly
liked Davis Tutt and his brother very much.

"That Remington I relieved you of earlier," he
said. "Do you know how to use it?"

"I was just a boy during most of the fighting," Davis said. "I missed out on the moral instruction that Lewis received, but I got an education of a different sort—I learned always to have a gun at hand, and to know how to use it. Tell me, Bill, how did you learn to shoot?"

"I hunted for game on the family farm since the time I could hold a rifle," he said. "Later, I went west and learned how to use a revolver."

"And what have you found to be the difference between killing rabbits and killing men?"

"The rabbits seldom shoot back," Hickok said.

Twenty-four

Storm clouds still filled the sky. It had rained for much of the night, and an occasional peal of thunder still shook the damp ground.

"'There shall be a time of trouble,'" Susannah Moore read, "'such as never was since there was a nation even to that same time: and at that time thy people shall be delivered, every one that shall be found written in the book.'"

She closed the Bible and looked over the several dozen mourners. She brushed away a wisp of hair from her face and continued from memory.

"'And many of them that sleep in the dust of the earth shall awake,'" she said in a fine and clear voice, "'some to everlasting life, and some to shame and everlasting contempt. And they that be wise shall shine as the brightness of the firmament, and they that turn many to righteousness, as the stars for ever and ever.'"

Then Davis Tutt knelt and scooped up a handful of red dirt. He weighed the dirt in his palm for a moment, then tossed it into the grave. The dirt struck the lid of the coffin with a hollow, skittering sound.

"Good-bye, Mother," he said.

Hickok and other men removed their coats, took up their shovels, and began to fill in the grave. The other mourners drew back, allowing the men room to work.

The cemetery was on the side of a hill overlooking Yellville, not far from an old church beside a huge oak tree. Vines covered the rough stone foundation of the church and crept up the whitewashed sides, and the cross atop the steeple was at a slightly skewed angle. Broad limestone steps led to the entrance, where the double oak doors stood open. Behind the church was a cabin with a wide porch, upon which rested an empty rocking chair.

Susannah Moore stood with Davis Tutt at the foot of the grave as the men toiled, her arm through his. Tears ran down his face as he watched. When at last the grave was filled, Susannah led Tutt toward the church. The men picked up their shovels, threw their jackets over their shoulders, and followed.

Inside, the women had piled tables with food, but nobody was eating yet.

Hickok was uncomfortable as only a stranger could be in a church full of people who had known one another all of their lives. Those who weren't clustered around Davis Tutt, placing hands on his shoulder and offering low words of comfort, were in small groups of their own, making conversation about the weather, the war, and town gossip. As they talked, they sometimes darted glances in Hickok's direction.

Hickok cleared his throat and ambled casually toward a doorway at the back of the sanctuary. He expected the door to lead outside, but when he opened it he found himself in an office. The walls were covered with calendars from the 1840s, and Millerite broadsheets, and quotations from the Book of Daniel written in a precise hand. Against a wall was a rolltop desk, and above the desk was a painting, done carefully but with little artistic merit, showing the end of the world. There was a cluster of people in white robes clustered around a church on a hill, which Hickok recognized as the church in which he now stood, except the cross atop the steeple was straight. Above the church, the cloudy heavens had split open and a river of fire was pouring toward the earth. The fire was mixed with falling stars, with points that numbered from five to seven. Angels blowing trumpets heralded the imminent cataclysm.

"My father had quite an imagination," Susannah Moore said as she stepped into the room. "I was just a child at the time of the Disappointments, but I remember how he spent days in this room, reading the Bible and scouring the newspapers for signs. And always, he was obsessed with time—calendars, clocks, watches."

"I prefer my art to be a little more cheerful," Hickok said. "Didn't you say he gave up this nonsense after the world failed to end the second time?"

"He never considered it nonsense," she said. "But he kept these things to remind him that it is not for us to know the hour of judgment."

"It seems cruel," Hickok said gently, "to inflict this philosophy on a child."

"I was terrified," she said, then laughed. "At least, I was the first time I put on the robe and stood in the October mist waiting for Christ to come down from the heavens. By the second time I was simply cold, because I knew what to expect—nothing."

Then she smiled.

"But my father was a gentle man," she said, "And even then I knew there were much worse things that men do to their children."

"You must have been a precocious child."

"Not so precocious," she said. "I was eight years old and could do a little reasoning on my own. It's not that I rejected prophecy, just man's imperfect reading of it. I still have nightmares, however, of being barefoot on this hillside—and seeing father's painting come to life."

"So you are now—"

"Twenty-five," she said defensively.

"No," he said. "I was going to ask if you are now the sole caretaker of your father's church."

"Oh, we have circuit preachers often enough, and singing on Saturdays and for funerals, and the congregation continues, such as it is," she said. "But yes, I take care of the church—poorly. It needs much work."

"It looks solid enough."

Susannah began opening drawers in the desk, inspecting the contents with a smile.

"The steeple," she said. "Did you not notice?"

"I noticed," he said. "It would seem easy enough to straighten."

She drew a pocket watch from one of the drawers.

"The men have offered," she said, "but I prefer it remain that way. On the night my father died, a terrible storm struck the town. The wind and the lightning were fierce, and several buildings were knocked down. The courthouse lost part of its roof. It was a little like what Father might have imagined the end of the world would have felt and sounded like, so I have left the cross alone."

"Why?"

Susannah rubbed the lid of the watch with her thumb.

"As a reminder that the path to heaven is seldom straight," she said. "Or perhaps to suggest an element of doubt—I don't know."

She replaced the watch in the drawer and slowly closed it. Then she smiled and grasped Hickok's arm.

"Join us," she said. "It is time to sing."

The congregation had arranged the pews and chairs in the sanctuary so that they sat in a square, facing one another across an empty space that was about ten feet across.

"Sit here," Susannah said, thrusting an old book of hymns into his hand and placing him in the back, with some of the other men and a few of the older children. Then she threaded her way to the open space and, with a hymnal in one hand, looked over the expectant faces.

"Suffield," she said. "Page one thirteen."

Then she held her right hand up and sang, "Fa."

The congregation attempted to match the pitch.

Susannah shook her head and sang the note again. Her voice was powerful and true, and Hickok could not help but think she had the voice of an angel. But then he decided that even that tired metaphor, which Susannah gave new life, fell far short. The timbre of her voice was perfection itself, the standard by which all things feminine were to be measured.

When the congregation had the note, she repeated the process twice more, singing "sol" and "la." When she was satisfied that everyone had found the key, she paused, her right hand raised.

Then she plunged her hand toward the floor and began to sing, and the congregation sang with her. Keeping time with her right hand, she looked from face to face, and a harmony that was both frightening in its volume and undeniable in its power filled the church.

"'Teach me the measure of my days,'" the congregation sang, "'thou maker of my frame. I would survey life's narrow space and learn how frail I am.'"

The bass notes thumped against Hickok's chest as the melody rang in his ears. It seemed to him as if the church itself had become an instrument, a sound box that amplified the dozens of voices just as the body of a violin magnified the sound of a bow upon its strings.

"'See the vain race of mortals move, like shadows o'er the plain. They rage and strive, desire and love, but all the noise is vain.'"

The members of the congregation began stamping their feet in time, adding to the power of the old hymn. The sound was so intense that it verged on the uncomfortable, but as it continued, it began to have a peculiar effect on Hickok; he breathed deeply, and his heart, which he had held clenched to the world for so long, began to loosen. His body resonated with the music, just as the old church was vibrating, and emotions rose up from the pit of his stomach. With his palm, he wiped tears from the corners of his eyes.

"'Some walk in honor's gaudy show, some dig for golden ore. They toil for heirs they know not who and straight are seen no more. Now I forbid my carnal hope, my fond desires recall; I give my mortal int'rest up, and make my God my all.'"

Then there was silence, and the silence was as powerful as the music had been.

Susannah smiled.

"Who will lead the next song?" she asked. "Davis?"

Davis Tutt came slowly from his chair and took Susannah's place in the hollow square. He thumbed through the pages of the songbook, *The Missouri Harmony*, but seemed undecided.

"'New Britain,'" he said at last.

Then he began to cry.

"I'm sorry," he said.

Susannah went to him and placed her arm around his waist.

"There is nothing to be ashamed of," she said.

"Look," cried a woman who was seated against the row of open windows on the east side of the church. "Have you ever seen anything so beautiful?"

Davis Tutt laid the songbook on a chair and made his way to the open window, where he placed his hands upon the sill and looked out.

In the sky beyond the cemetery was a perfect rainbow.

Twenty-five

Hickok sat in a straight-backed chair on the porch of the saloon, his boots propped on the rail and his hat pulled low over his eyes. Sweat dripped from his chin onto his shirt. His hands were folded over his stomach, and within reach on the porch was a glass of water.

Davis Tutt came out of the saloon, a bottle of whiskey in his hand. He dragged a chair over to Hickok, sat down, and tipped the bottle toward Hickok's water.

Hickok put a hand over the glass.

"I'm comfortable," he said.

"Don't spoil the fun," Tutt said. "Have a drink."

"Nobody's stopping you," Hickok said. "Get blind drunk if that's what you want. But I told you, I'm comfortable."

"Get religion?" Tutt asked.

"Go to hell," Hickok said.

"Susannah can have that effect on a man," Tutt said, then took a swig from the bottle. "I went on the wagon for nearly a year because of her. Now I prefer my spirits from Kentucky."

"Given up on her?"

"She gave up on me," he said. "We are both much less frustrated."

"Is either of you any happier?"

"Jim," Tutt said, "I'm a naturally happy man. At least, until I'm unhappy, and then there's hell to pay. I just don't know who to whip to make me feel better about my mother, so I guess I'll just take it out on myself."

He took another long drink.

"That's a foolish plan," Hickok said.

"But it's a plan, and that's what counts."

Hickok pushed the hat back, wiped the sweat from his face with a sleeve, and took a drink of water as he surveyed the street. The mud had dried into hard ruts, and the weather-beaten storefronts radiated heat. The afternoon sun was low in the sky, and its brilliance glinted from the windows of the courthouse across the street. From the woods at the edge of town, near Crooked Creek, the locusts had begun their ululating chorus.

"This is a nice town," Hickok said. "Restful."

"I'm weary of it."

"But weary can be a comfortable feeling," Hickok said. "Everybody in town knows you, and most of them like you, evidently, from the turnout at the funeral."

"They liked my mother," he said.

"Funerals aren't for the dead," Hickok said. "They're for those the dead leave behind. You can't buy friends like that, Dave—they must be earned."

Tutt grinned, took another drink, and wiped his mouth with the back of his hand.

"That boy, Jackson," Hickok said. "He looks up to you."

"Well, that's a ringing endorsement—the son of the town drunk. Jackson's not even his name. It's his father's name. He is Jack's son. Pretty soon that just became Jackson, and everybody forgot what he was supposed to be called."

"Where is the old man?"

"Who knows?" Tutt said, and waved his hand at the horizon. "Sleeping off the last drunk somewhere, I imagine. It's better that way. Jackson receives his fury when the old man is around and sober."

"Why do you allow it?"

"Why do you think?"

"You believe children are a man's personal property, to abuse as he sees fit?"

"You do see things in black and white, don't you?"

"What do you mean?"

"Some problems aren't easy to solve," Tutt said. "Consider the consequences if I take exception the

next time the old man beats the hell out of Jackson.
Blows just don't stay where you land them. They
spread. I can beat the sorry bastard like an old rug,
but he'll just take it out on the boy that much
harder when I'm not around. And then you have
the problem of Jackson seeing his father shamed in
front of him—no boy wants to see that. And do
you think I would feel good about whipping a
drunk who is twice my age and half my weight?"

"Still," Hickok said.

"No, there's only one person that can rectify the
situation," Tutt said. "The boy is getting bigger
now, and one of these days he's going to have to
decide to take his whipping like a dog or stand up
for himself. When that time comes, all those beat-
ings that Jackson has choked down will come back
up like a bad piece of meat."

"It's not a pretty thought," Hickok said.

"No, it's easier to think in black and white, ain't
it? Besides, you're the one he favors now, Jim."

"My friends call me Bill," Hickok said. He was
watching the end of the street, where the trees
leaned low, creating an arch filled with the drowsy
afternoon light—and framing a wagon pulled by a
team of mules.

"Know that rig?" Hickok asked.

Tutt turned to look while lifting the bottle.

Hickok snatched the whiskey away.

Tutt started to protest, but was distracted by the

sight of the wagon, which was flanked by two riders who held their long guns at the ready.

"They do look deliberate, don't they?"

"Go inside and fetch the iron," Hickok said.

While Tutt was inside, Hickok took a pull from the whiskey. Tutt came back out a moment later, cradling a double-barreled shotgun and carrying Hickok's revolvers by a finger looped through the trigger guards.

Hickok took the guns, checked the cylinders, then placed them butt forward in his belt. Tutt leaned against the doorframe and held the shotgun, barrels down, in his right hand.

The wagon drew to a stop in front of the saloon.

The riders were young men who, in their filthy clothes and wild heads of black hair, might have been mirror images of each other. One of them held an old plains rifle in his right hand, and the other had an ugly, short-barreled musket.

The old man driving the wagon had a bald crown and dirty white hair that tumbled down to the shoulders of his filthy brown shirt. He had a thick beard, and a clay pipe was clenched in his teeth.

He took the pipe out of his mouth and spit upon the ground, then took a greasy paper sack of tobacco from his pocket. He took his time filling the pipe.

Hickok and Tutt waited.

The old man pulled a match across the wagon seat, then regarded the flame.

"I'm looking for my boys," he said, then lit the pipe.

"Looking for trouble is more like it," Tutt said.

The old man flipped the match into the street.

"Son, we don't look for trouble. We are trouble."

Hickok stared at the old man.

"Those your sons as well?" Hickok asked.

"Handsome, ain't they?"

"I'll yield the point," Hickok said. "Ask them to put the guns in the back of the wagon, and then all three of you move along. We can't help you."

"Now, that's where we differ," the old man said. "You see, I understand my two youngest are lying dead in that livery. Are they in there, mister?"

Hickok was silent.

"Well?" the old man demanded.

"The men who were in that livery were road agents," Tutt said. "We didn't know their names. Nobody came for them, so we put them in the ground."

"You had no right to bury 'em," the old man said.

"They weren't keeping in the heat," Hickok said.

"You had no right," the old man said.

"We can put up markers with their proper names," Tutt said. "Who were they?"

"Wouldn't you like to know," the old man said,

then sneered. "Their names are known only to us, and we will not tolerate strangers to hold their names in the same filthy mouths that spread lies about them."

"They were robbers," Hickok said.

"How do you know?"

"I was there," he said. "They tried to rob the coach, and they killed the driver in the process. The fact that it is unpleasant to contemplate makes it no less true."

"Who killed 'em?"

Hickok was silent.

"Your eyes betray you," the old man said.

"If you won't give us their names or yours," Tutt said, "then our business is done."

"Far from done!" the old man shouted. "Far from done. The tall one has murdered my children. Why isn't he in the jail yonder?"

"There was no murder," Tutt said.

"So says he," the old man said. "So says he."

"What do you want?" Hickok asked.

"Many things," the old man said. "But today, I will take my children home."

"It's like my friend already told you," Hickok said. "They are in the ground."

"They can be taken out of the ground."

"That is a morbid thought," Hickok said.

"Less so than leaving them with strangers," the old man said. "How do we know you didn't feed them to the hogs or just toss their bodies into that creek?"

"They eat their own hogs," Hickok said, "and their water comes from the creek. Your boys were treated with respect, even though they had not earned it. Leave the dead in peace."

"You can ask me nothing," the old man said. "It is we who will do the telling."

Then he waved a gnarled hand, and his boys cocked their weapons. Tutt brought up the shotgun and slowly drew back both hammers.

"My boy's musket is filled with tacks," the old man said. "Hell, he can probably get both of you where you stand. And my other boy has a ball the size of your thumb ready, if one of you survives."

"Put down the shotgun, Dave," Hickok said. He had not made a motion toward his revolvers.

"Like hell I will," Tutt said.

"This is a bad situation gone to hell," Hickok said. "There isn't any sense in all of us getting slaughtered over a couple of corpses. What's the harm in letting them have the bodies?"

"They're not taking them at the point of a gun."

"If they put down their guns," Hickok said, "can they have them?"

"I reckon."

"What about it, old man?"

"I allow," he said.

He waved his hand at his sons, and they lowered their weapons.

"Put them in the wagon," Tutt said over the shotgun.

They urged their horses over to the wagon, then carefully placed the guns in the bed.

Tutt lowered the shotgun.

"I reckon we need some shovels," the old man said.

Twenty-six

As the moon rose in the east, Hickok raised the bail of the lamp and thrust a match to the wick, which ignited with a soft popping sound. Hickok tossed the match to the dirt and ground it with the heel of his boot, then swung the lantern over the grave.

While his two wild-looking sons toiled in the grave, the old man sat nearby, smoking his clay pipe and occasionally barking a word of encouragement or displeasure at their progress. On the opposite side of the grave was a huge mound of dirt and stones, and amid the clods writhed purple and black earthworms and white grubs. The mound grew with each shovelful of dirt that was thrown from the grave.

Hickok hung the lantern from a low branch of a nearby tree, while Tutt cradled the shotgun in his left arm and removed a pair of cigars from his vest pocket.

"Don't light it yet," Tutt said, as Hickok took one of the cigars.

"Have you hit any wood?" the old man asked.

"There's no wood," Tutt said.

"My sons weren't good enough for boxes?"

"Some kind words were said over them," Tutt said. "It seemed generous at the time."

The men who were in the grave looked even wilder than before. Their clothes were now smeared with clay, and mud was clotted in their hair. Their face and arms shone with sweat, and mad eyes flashed in their dark faces.

Then the blade of one of their shovels struck something that sounded like a wet burlap sack, and soon both of them were pulling a corpse, by one limp arm, from the dirt. Then one of the wild men released the limb and turned his face, gagging.

"Throw me your kerchief, Pa," he said.

"Don't act like a damned split tail," the old man said. "Keep working and get your poor dead brothers out of that hole."

The horrid smell reached Hickok's nostrils, and he put the cigar in his mouth and drew a match. He ignited the match in the chimney of the lantern, lit the cigar, and passed the match to Tutt.

The night wind curled the smoke over their shoulders.

The first body was deposited at the lip of the grave, where it rolled over onto its back. The old man gasped when he saw that the corpse had no face.

"Who mutilates human beings in such a way?" he asked, his voice shaking with rage.

"He did it to himself," Hickok said. "He dropped a shotgun beneath his chin during the fight, and that was the result."

"Shame," the old man said.

The wild ones were bringing the other body out of the grave when Hickok heard footsteps behind them, and he pulled both of his revolvers as he turned.

"It's me," Susannah said. "I saw the lantern from the cabin, and could hear the shovels. I feared it was grave robbers."

"Go back," Hickok said as he returned the guns to his belt.

Susannah stepped forward into the light.

"They're taking their dead," Hickok said as he draped an arm around her and drew her back. "Please, this is no place for you."

"Ah," the old man said, his milky eyes wide. "You have no small feeling for this woman. A sister, perhaps? A sweetheart?"

"Shut up," Tutt said.

"Go back to the cabin," Hickok urged. "They have promised to leave as soon as they have the bodies loaded on their wagon."

"It's late." The old man sniffed. "We've not ate."

"You have what you came for," Tutt said. "And you're leaving directly."

"This doesn't feel right," Susannah said as Hickok led her away. "Opening graves in the middle of the night? There should be a preacher here, at least—"

"We don't want these men to become too comfortable," Hickok said. "They've already seen too much. Go back and bar your door until morning. Better yet, come stay at the saloon tonight."

"I have never spent a night in a saloon," Susannah said, "and I will not take up the practice now. Why didn't you tell me what was going on down here?"

"I was hoping to have this conversation after the clan with no name had left."

"What do you mean, 'no name'?"

"They wouldn't give us their names or where they're from," Hickok said. "They are rough men, too rough for this fair little town."

When Hickok returned to the grave, the second body was lying beside the first, with the wild ones standing over them. They threw their shovels onto the mound of dirt.

"Fill it in," Tutt said.

"What?"

"Fill in the hole," Tutt said. "It will raise too many questions in the morning if folks discover the grave has been opened. I'm not in the mood to enlighten folks about what has happened here tonight."

"Pa!" one of the sons cried.

"Do it," the old man said.

They wearily took up the shovels.

Tutt drew Hickok a few yards away, then whispered in his ear: "Perhaps we shouldn't allow them to leave."

"What do you mean?" Hickok asked.

"The grave is already open," Tutt said. "Perhaps we should fill it with all of them."

Hickok stared at him.

"They are unarmed," he said.

"They would cut our throats if they thought they could get away with it," Tutt said. "Besides, do you think this will end after they drive out of town?"

"That worries me as well," Hickok said. "But we gave our word."

"What do you think *their* word is worth?" Tutt whispered.

"I don't know," Hickok said, "but I do know what mine is worth."

Tutt shook his head.

"Hey, what are you gabbing about over there?" the old man called. "You are a couple of old slits, whispering to each other like that. Are you thinking you should kill us where we stand, while you have the chance?"

"That notion had presented itself," Hickok said.

The wild ones stopped their work and looked at their father with alarm.

Tutt cocked the shotgun.

"Keep shovelin'," the old man barked.

He rapped his pipe with the heel of his hand, and the ashes spilled on the ground. Then he turned to Hickok and Tutt and gave them a broad smile.

"Ha!" he said. "I'd kill us, if the situation was reversed. But you can't. Don't have the oysters for it, do you?"

"Don't be so sure," Tutt said. The butt of the shotgun was on his thigh, and his right forefinger was in the trigger guard.

"The trouble ends here," Hickok said.

"No trouble," the old man said easily.

"Swear on the souls of your dead sons," Tutt urged.

The old man's face clouded for a moment.

"No need for either of you to fear for your persons," he said. "There will be no gunshots, no knives flashing in the moonlight, no stones brought down upon unsuspecting skulls. When we leave here we will never return—for any reason. By my blood that has watered your undeserving ground, I swear it."

Twenty-seven

Hickok wearily followed Tutt into the saloon. Tutt placed the shotgun on the bar as Hickok fell into one of the chairs around one of the round poker tables. He took off his hat, placed it on the table, and rubbed his face with his hands.

Sunlight was streaming in from the windows facing the street.

Tutt took a bottle from beneath the bar, uncorked it with his teeth, and poured two glasses half-full of whiskey. Then he carried the glasses over to the table, where he sat down opposite Hickok and pushed one of the glasses toward him.

"To your health," Tutt said, then drained the glass in one pull.

"I'm too tired to drink," Hickok said.

"That is tired indeed," Tutt said, pushing the empty glass aside and taking up the one that

Hickok had refused. "I intend to sleep for a couple of days, at least."

"Keep drinking like that and you will," Hickok said.

"I don't think I'll ever get that smell out of my nostrils," Tutt said. "Don't think I've ever smelled anything like it."

Jackson burst through the doorway.

"Come quick," he said. "Fire—Miss Moore's cabin is ablaze."

By noon, the cabin had been reduced to a pile of smoking ashes beneath a blackened chimney. The fire had been so intense that, by the time Hickok and Tutt reached it, the buckets of water they threw upon it simply disappeared in clouds of steam. Hickok had attempted to enter the cabin, but Tutt—along with some of the other men who had come to help—had restrained him.

"What now?" Tutt asked.

Hickok stood twenty yards from what remained of the cabin, but the heat still seared his face his hands. He turned away.

"There must have been others," Hickok said. "We should have known."

"We followed the rig out of town," Tutt said. "Then we went back and checked on Susannah just before dawn. If only she had agreed to come to town with us."

"Do you think—"

"I don't know," Hickok said. "It will be tomorrow before these ashes are cool enough to sift. With a fire that intense, there might not be much left to find—some teeth, perhaps. Or we could sift for days and come to the conclusion that they took her and burned the cabin to keep us busy."

"So what are you saying?"

"If she's still alive, she needs us to be on the trail now," Hickok said. "And if she's not alive, we don't have long to find that rig and take our revenge. Either way, the result is going to be the same—there will be killing, and it will be easier for us if we can catch them on the road, before they hole up in whatever snake pit they call home."

"Jackson," Tutt called.

"Yes, sir?" the boy said.

"Run to the livery and tell them to get our horses saddled. Then put together whatever grub you can find, double quick, and put it in the saddle wallets."

"You two are going alone?" the boy asked. "Shouldn't you wait until some of the other men can saddle up as well?"

"We need to travel fast," Hickok said. "We don't have time to wait for a posse. Besides, who else in town do you think has the talent required for this sort of thing? Every man who knew how to use a gun is now someplace in Missouri, fighting the Yankees."

"I can go," Jackson said.

"You're not going," Hickok and Tutt said in unison.

Jackson looked hurt.

"I know you want to help," Hickok said. "But you're not old enough yet."

"What about Mister Lewis?" Jackson asked.

"After we're gone, tell him," Tutt said, "but not before. My brother has a good heart, but he doesn't know one end of a gun from another. Besides, he has a family to look after."

Jackson nodded.

"Now go," Hickok said.

Jackson took off running.

"The boy has a point," Tutt said. "If the rest of the clan is anything like the three we've already seen, we are as good as dead and gone to hell."

"I don't care," Hickok said.

"Well, if Susannah is alive—and I'm not sure even to hope for it, thinking about what those animals might do to her—then we're not going to help her by getting ourselves killed."

"Stay, then," Hickok said. "But I don't have a choice—I'm the one who brought this trouble to town, and it is my obligation to fix it, if I can."

Tutt laughed.

"Hell, cousin, there's no way I'm sitting this out," he said. "Susannah is as dear to me as family, and whatever they've done to her, I aim to put a few of those stinking sonsabitches in the ground.

But the problem is, we don't even know which way to ride. They came into town from one direction and left in another."

Hickok looked at him.

"Ever hear of the White River Mill?"

Twenty-eight

They reached the mill after two days and one night of hard riding. It was a rambling and weather-beaten old building, built hard against a bluff, and it drew power for the wheel from a spring that gushed from the hillside and eventually joined the White River below.

"You know the miller?" Hickok asked as he looped the reins around the hitching rail.

"I said I knew where the mill was," Tutt said. "I didn't say anything about knowing the people. Most folks in the Ozarks never get more than fifteen or twenty miles away from home in their entire lives."

"The war will change that," Hickok said.

"Don't you think we would have caught up with the wagon by now if they were headed this way?" Tutt asked wearily. "We had to be making twice their speed."

"Depends on exactly where they live," Hickok said. "We crossed a dozen trails on the way, and any one of them could be a shorter route home."

The pair brushed the dust from their clothes as they walked up the steps to the mill's long porch. They found the miller sitting on a barrel just outside the entrance. He was a small man with a scruffy beard and thinning hair, and he looked at the pair with distrust as they approached.

"Haven't seen you before," he said curtly.

"Not surprised," Hickok said. "We've never been here before."

"That explains it."

Tutt swung open the door and peered inside the mill.

"I'm alone, if that's what you're checking," the miller said. "What the hell do you want?"

Hickok pulled the grain sack from his pocket and showed it to the man.

"This come from your mill?"

"It says so, don't it?" the man asked. "I reckon those stains are blood."

"You guess correctly," Hickok said, and stuffed the sack back into his pocket. "We're looking for a filthy old man with long white hair and two wild-looking sons of better than average size. Know anybody like that in these parts?"

"You the law?"

"No," Hickok said.

"Then who's askin'?"

"So you know them," Tutt said.

"Didn't say that," the miller said.

"You didn't have to," Tutt said. "Look, we don't have time to explain ourselves. Tell us what you know, while we're still asking you friendly."

"I'm not disposed to cater to strangers asking questions," the man said.

"I say we beat it out of him," Tutt said.

"If we have to," Hickok said.

"Better start beating," the miller said. "I can survive a whipping, but if I tell you what you want to know, I'm a dead man. The folks you seek are a private lot, and they have killed for less."

"So you're afraid," Hickok said.

"Slow, ain't you?"

"Let me explain this so you can understand," Hickok said. "These men you know have killed or kidnapped a friend of ours, a girl, and by helping us you will be doing the right thing."

"Doing the right thing pays poorly."

"So that's it?" Hickok asked. "You want money?"

"What do you reckon my life's worth?"

"Dave, give me your money," Hickok said.

"Like hell," Tutt said. "A beating is cheaper."

"Give me your money," Hickok repeated.

Tutt cursed, but withdrew a gold coin from his pocket and handed it to Hickok.

"Look here," Hickok said, holding the coin in front of the miller's face. "This is ten dollars gold. It's all we have, so there's no point in bargaining for more. Give up what we need, and this is yours."

"The old man's name is Heskett Deaver, and he's a power doctor. He and his brood have lived at Hog Scald for as long as anyone can remember," the miller said. He reached for the coin.

Hickok closed his fist around it.

"Where's Hog Scald?"

"Give me the money," the miller said. "I told you what you wanted to know."

Tutt leaned down and whispered in the man's ear, "But that's not all you know, is it?"

"Where's Hog Scald?" Hickok asked.

"Three hollers south," he said.

"How many sons does the old man have?"

"Seven."

"Does that count the two dead ones?"

"That would make five," the miller said.

"Anybody else live with them?" Tutt asked. "Wives, children, anybody?"

"The old woman died sudden a few winters back—some say Heskett killed her in a fit of rage for curdling his magic, or trying to. None of the sons are married. When they see a woman they want, the story is, they just go out and take her."

"What kind of place is it?" Hickok asked.

"Imagine the most wretched you can imagine, and it's worse."

"No, is it wood or brick or—"

"Stone," the miller said. "The house is stone, and it's built atop a ridge at the far end of the holler. There are some stock pens and such around it, and heavy woods, and there's just one way in or out—the road that leads right up the draw."

Hickok opened his palm. The man snatched away the coin.

"What's a power doctor?" Hickok asked.

"Kind of a witch," Tutt said. "They claim to be able to cure people by mumbling stuff over them and giving them charms and such."

"You believe that kind of truck?" Tutt asked.

"I don't know what to believe," the miller said. "But they say Heskett Deaver was filled with remorse after killing his wife, and raised her from the dead, but had to murder her all over again because she weren't human."

"What rubbish," Tutt said.

"If crops go bad in these parts or somebody's hog wanders off or a normally healthy child falls sick, they blame Deaver. Makes as much sense as anything else, I reckon. So, two of his sons are dead?"

"Killed while trying to rob a coach," Tutt said. "The old man came to town and had a couple of his boys dig them out of the cemetery. Said they were going to take the bodies home for burial."

"So it must be true what they say."

"What's true?"

"That the old man would never allow any of his sons to be buried in consecrated ground," the miller said. "When Heskett Deaver is called home to hell, he wants to have his boys close at hand to help fight off that hag of a wife he sent before."

Twenty-nine

"What do you think?" Tutt asked.
They lay upon their bellies at the crest of the ridge, guns in hand, looking down upon the rock house below. It was more of a fortress than a house, with thick walls and narrow windows and little cover in the dirt yard around it. The horses were in a split-rail pen out back, and the old wagon was hard against the house on one side.

"It seems unnaturally quiet," Hickok said. "They're home, because there is smoke coming out of the chimney. I would have expected the old man to have his sons guarding the outside, but I don't see anything."

"Why did it have to be rock?" Tutt asked. "They could hole up in there for a week and we couldn't flush them out."

"We don't have a week," Hickok said, then

reached up into the branches of the tree overhead and touched a charm made of sticks and feathers. "They have a peculiar way of decorating."

"Probably some conjure against strangers," Tutt said. "We could wait here and hope to catch them in the yard, then kill them."

"They're not going to come out all at once."

"But if they do have Susannah, and we storm the house, they'll kill her."

"We have to assume she's already dead."

"So, what's the plan?"

"The windows are too narrow to get through, even if we could reach them unseen, and if we rushed them, we'd be dead before we got to the front door. No, there has to be some way to make them come to us."

"Ordinarily I'd say burn them out, but rock don't burn. Even the damned roof looks like it's made of slab."

"Then we use something besides fire," Hickok said.

"Like what?"

Hickok looked around the hillside.

"Like that," Hickok said, and nodded toward a hornet's nest in one of the trees.

"Are you touched?"

"Have a better idea?" Hickok asked.

"Well, no. But maybe if I thought about it a while . . ."

"No time," Hickok said. "We do this now, while

there is still plenty of daylight. I don't want to be trading shots with them in the dark."

"This should be interesting," Tutt said.

Hickok climbed over the wagon and onto the roof, the nest buzzing in a blanket beneath his arm. Beneath him, he could hear the voices of the men in the cabin, sometimes punctuated by a coarse laugh.

He did not hear a woman's voice.

The gaps between the stone slabs had been filled with clay, and offered no glimpse of the interior. He crept across the roof to the chimney, then paused for a moment of concentration. He drew away the blanket and, grasping the nest in both hands, threw it as hard as he could down the chimney. He hardly felt the hornets that stung him on his face and hands.

He heard the nest as it bounced off the sides and then landed with a hollow breaking sound on the logs below, followed by a furious swarming. Then there were shouts and curses, and he drew his revolvers as he ran over the peak of the roof to wait over the front door.

The wooden door burst open, and a boy of twenty staggered out, swatting hornets with one hand and clutching a rifle in the other.

Davis Tutt emerged from behind a stump at the edge of the yard, pointed his Remington, and fired.

The boy fell, but still struggled with the rifle.

Hickok jumped from the roof to the ground, put a ball into the back of the wounded boy's head, then rushed for the open door. Inside the cabin he could see the startled eyes of a man as he rushed for the door as well. The man got his shoulder behind the door just as Hickok reached it, and they struggled with the planks sandwiched between them, the smoking revolver in Hickok's right hand.

Then a rifle ball splintered the wood a couple of inches from Hickok's shoulder.

"Damn you!" Hickok bellowed.

Tutt ran and hurled himself at the door, knocking backward the man holding it shut. The rifle dropped from his hands, but as he hit the ground, he drew a knife from his belt. He lunged with the blade as Hickok stepped through the door. Hickok kicked the knife out of his hand and pointed one of the Navies at the man's face.

"Where are the others?" Hickok demanded.

The man was about thirty years old, and he had the same coarse black hair as the other Deaver sons. His mouth opened and closed, but no sound came out.

"Tell me!" Hickok said, and cocked the revolver.

The man clasped his hands together, pleading.

"Kill him," Tutt urged.

Hickok could feel his temples throbbing in time to his heartbeat, and there was a rushing in his ears. The room was dark and filled with angry hornets, and Hickok batted the insects away as he peered into the gloom. The room stank. Suddenly Hickok's vision narrowed, and the room became even darker, and he staggered a bit.

"Bill?" Tutt asked.

"Open the door wide," Hickok said. "Get some light in here and let some of these damned hornets out."

Tutt turned and kicked the door so hard that it jammed open. The room was flooded with sunlight, revealing piles of dirty rags, furs, stacks of animal bones, antlers, and half-eaten plates of food swarming with flies.

"Do you have the girl?" Hickok asked.

The man on the floor remained silent, but his eyes were filled with tears. He glanced at the closed door that led to the back room.

Tutt put a finger to his lips.

Hickok nodded.

Tutt pointed angrily at the man on the floor, telling him without words to stay put, and he followed Hickok to the door. Hickok drew his leg back and kicked the door inward; then both of them turned away as a musket blast peppered the door with tacks and bits of glass, some of which bounced from the wood and raked Hickok's cheek. Then Hickok threw himself into the room, where he was confronted by one of the sons who had come to Yellville with the old man. As he dropped the musket and tried to pull a dragoon pistol from his belt, Hickok shot him three times in the chest. The man fell against the wall and sank to the floor, blood pouring from his nose and mouth.

On the bed was Susannah.

She was spread-eagled. Heavy leather straps were around her wrists and ankles, and she was gagged by a wadded rabbit pelt. She was in her nightclothes, which were stained and torn, and she had a broken nose and a black eye. Her nostrils were caked with dried blood, and she was having trouble breathing.

As Hickok drew his knife to cut Susannah free, there was a sound behind them. Tutt whirled, gun drawn, and found the silent man coming through the door with an ax. Tutt shot him in the chest. The man stopped, eyes blank, but did not go down or drop the ax. Then he staggered forward, and Tutt placed the muzzle of the Remington nearly against the man's forehead and pulled the trigger. The .45-caliber ball took away the back of the man's skull, and his body turned as he fell, presenting a gruesome scene of bone and pinkish material and matted hair.

The man sitting on the floor looked up.

"He was mute," he said through a mouthful of blood.

"Shut up," Hickok said, then drew his revolver and shot him again.

Then Hickok and Tutt looked at each other.

"Any more?" Hickok asked.

"I don't think so," Tutt said.

"Then help me," he said.

Hickok removed the gag from Susannah's mouth, and she gulped in air. Then Tutt, who had taken the knife from Hickok, began slashing the straps that held her down.

"Susannah," Hickok said. "Talk to me."

Susannah tried to speak, but could only cough.

"Where are the others?" he asked.

She shook her head, had another coughing spasm, then managed one word: "Water."

"There's nothing fit to drink here," Hickok said. "We're getting you out of here and then you can have all the water you want. Can you walk?"

Susannah nodded.

Hickok helped her out of bed and supported her with one arm while they left the back room and made for the front door. They crossed the main room, where a few hornets still buzzed, and then emerged into the sunlight of the yard.

"I reckon that's far enough," Heskett Deaver said.

He had been standing against the wall of the house on one side of the door, and his two remaining sons were standing on the other side. Heskett clutched a walking stick, but both of his sons held guns. The big wild one who had come to Yellville held a shotgun, and the other, smaller man—who had his right arm in a sling—was pointing a revolver.

"Drop your guns," the tall son said.

Hickok and Tutt extended their revolvers to arm's length.

"Easy," Haskett warned.

The pair dropped the revolvers into the dirt.

"The long-hair has another in his belt," Heskett said. "Take it."

While the tall one kept the shotgun trained on the trio, the short one tucked his own revolver into his belt and stepped forward to snatch the remaining Colt from Hickok's belt. Then he picked up the revolvers that were in the dirt.

"You're the one, ain't you?" he hissed through bad teeth.

"I'm the one what?" Hickok asked.

"The one what shot me," the short one said.

"Not nearly well enough, apparently."

Heskett Deaver stepped forward and brought his walking stick down on Hickok's skull. The blow made Hickok gasp and sag, but he did not fall.

"Shut the hell up," Heskett said, then flipped his white hair behind his shoulders. "You nearly got away, but you made a mistake—you should have shut the door behind you. If you had dragged poor Scotty inside"—here his milky eyes regarded the dead boy—"and shut the door, we would have approached without knowing anything was amiss, and you could have killed us at your leisure. But that open door just shouted that something was wrong, so we became cautious. You always have to keep your eyes on doors, because that's where heartache comes from."

"We'll do better next time," Tutt said.

The walking stick came down on his head.

"Luck was with you up until this last instant," Heskett said. "If the three of us had been inside, it would have been short work to deal with you. But you came when I decided to check the fish lines in the creek, and you caught the youngest and the dumbest at home. That's the funny thing about luck—it can change just like that."

"Let the girl go," Hickok said. "Keep us and kill us, if you like, but let her go."

"Oh, I will kill you, but why should I let the split go?" he asked. "She's the only one of you that interests me. She is a handsome one, isn't she? She'll make a fine bride for me . . . and my surviving boys."

"Never." Susannah gasped.

"Ever, I think," Heskett said, and laughed. "Ever."

She shook her head.

"Just looking at you makes me feel like a young man again." Heskett sighed. "Oh, how the sap begins to run and the tree grows proud."

"Let us go and we'll bring you money," Tutt said.

The walking stick came down again.

"Don't bargain with me as you would an imbecile," Heskett said. "I have what I want, and it is finally clear to me how one should treat a woman—and that is with the same regard that one would treat a hog. Only you can't eat a woman when you're finished with it."

"Are you sure, Pa?" the tall one asked.

Then all the Deavers laughed.

"Perhaps you're right," Heskett said with a smile. "We raise hogs for their flesh, so why not women?" He reached a hand out and grasped Susannah by the chin. "You would make a fine meal, wouldn't you? Now, there is one sin I've yet to try—guess you can say I've never had an appetite for it, until now."

"You're insane," Hickok said.

"Don't state the obvious," the old man said, then nodded at the tall one, who drove the butt of the shotgun into the small of Hickok's back.

Hickok fell to his hands and knees.

Susannah dropped to the ground beside him, her arm draped over his back.

"Is it time for the wedding, Pa?" the short one asked.

"Patience," Heskett said. "We must deal with this one and his friend first."

"Should I kill him now?" the tall one asked.

"Oh, he'll die, but it will be slow, so he'll have plenty of time to think about what he's done,"

Heskett said. "He's killed five of my sons, and a quick death is too good for him. What do you think is fitting?"

"We could chop a little bit off of him at a time, starting with his pecker, until he's dead," the short one said.

"We could boil him alive," the other one suggested.

"Those are pleasant thoughts," Heskett said, "but I've got something else in mind. We'll skin him alive. We'll peel his hide like we skin a rabbit—except we'll do his slow and let him watch, and we'll pour salt in the raw flesh as we go along."

"That's grand," the tall one said. "I can't wait to see that."

"What about the other one?" the short son asked.

"We just kill him," Heskett said.

"Now?" The tall one cocked the shotgun.

"Suits me," Heskett said.

"Wait," Hickok said.

"What in hell for?" Heskett asked.

"If you're intent on shooting him, I have some words for him," Hickok said.

"You can talk to him while he takes off his clothes," Heskett said. "For that matter, you can both start shucking your duds. You both have fine clothes, and I hate to ruin them with blood and shit."

Hickok struggled to his feet and drew Susannah with him.

"All right," he said, and began to fumble with the buttons of his shirt.

"No," Susannah said.

"Be still," Hickok said. "You need to listen to this."

"I ain't taking off my clothes," Tutt said. "Shoot me where I stand."

"Boys," Heskett said, "one of you hack the lesser toes from that woman to convince him."

"Stop," Tutt said. "All right."

He began to unbutton as well.

"Dave, I'm sorry to have to tell you like this, but seeing as this is the end, I don't want to die without being square with you."

"What the hell are you talking about?"

"My name isn't Bass," Hickok said. "It's Hickok. I'm a Union scout."

"A spy?" Tutt asked.

"A poor one, it would seem."

Tutt laughed.

"Hell, that's okay—I'm a Confederate deserter."

"Men," Susannah mumbled, then said in a hoarse voice, "Both about to die and worried about whether you're still buddies. Don't you dare give up now."

Tutt tossed his shirt and vest on the ground. Hickok was already bare from the waist up and was removing his boots. When those were off, he started on his trousers and then his socks.

"Sorry," Hickok told Susannah.

"Please," she said.

"All right, both of you—on your knees," Heskett said.

Susannah began to whisper the Lord's Prayer.

"Shut that mouth," Heskett said, "or we'll shut it for you."

She stopped.

Hickok and Tutt knelt. Both were nude.

"All right, the one to die quick—hands on your head."

Tutt laced his fingers behind his neck.

"Do it," Heskett said.

The tall one stood behind Tutt, and he carefully shouldered the shotgun. As he brought the muzzle down toward the top of Tutt's head, his index finger snaked inside the trigger guard.

"Make it count," Tutt said.

Then a shot rang out, and the tall one staggered back, looking disbelievingly at the hole in his chest. Hickok pushed Susannah to the ground while Tutt came to his feet and snatched the shotgun away from the tall one.

The short one fumbled to cock the revolver, and Tutt, following the motion with the shotgun, pulled both triggers.

The blast took away the hand at the wrist.

The man stared at the bloody stump and screamed.

Tutt gripped the barrels of the empty shotgun and, swinging it like a bat, hit the short one in the mouth. He went down, and Tutt continued to beat him with the butt of the gun until he was sure he was dead.

Then Tutt turned to the tall one. He was already dead.

The old man started toward one of Hickok's revolvers, which lay on the ground. Hickok sprang for it and reached it first, but as he brought the gun up, the old man knocked it from his hand with the walking stick.

He had lifted the stick for another blow when a voice commanded him to stop.

"Just back off," said Lewis Tutt from twenty yards away. He had reloaded the carbine he had used to kill the tall one and was now looking over its sights at the old man.

"A nigger," Heskett Deaver said. "Bested by a nigger."

"I don't like that word," Lewis Tutt said.

"Good to see you, brother. How'd you find us?"

"Jackson," Lewis said. "And the miller."

The boy emerged from behind Lewis, his eyes wide.

"Go back," Hickok said as he picked the nearest Navy from the ground.

The boy saw the other revolver on the ground,

near the old man, and he reached to get it for Hickok.

In one motion, Heskett Deaver pulled a razor from his waistband and grabbed the boy by the hair on the back of his head. He pulled the boy to him, shielding him from the .50-caliber carbine.

Jackson grimaced and cried out.

Hickok fired, sending a ball into the old man's right eye. As he fell, the razor slashed down below Jackson's nose, splitting both lips. The boy fell to the ground, holding his mouth, blood pouring from between his fingers.

Hickok stepped forward and emptied the revolver into the old man's head, which shattered like a pumpkin.

Lewis dropped the carbine and held the boy by the shoulders.

"Let me see," he said.

"No," Jackson mumbled.

"Move your hands," Lewis urged.

The boy dropped his hands. His front teeth glinted behind the mutilated lips, while blood gushed down his chin.

"It's ugly," Lewis said, "but you'll live."

The boy began to cry.

"I'm sorry," Lewis said as he hugged the boy. "I'm sorry I let you come."

"I just wanted to help," the boy said.

"You did," Hickok said. He had pulled his trousers on by now, and he put his hand on the boy's shoulder. "You saved us. We'd be dead if you hadn't told Lewis. You were the smart one."

"I didn't know what to do," Jackson said. "Mister Davis said he couldn't shoot."

"He can't," Davis Tutt said, hopping on one leg as he pulled on his pants. "That was a miracle shot. I'm lucky he didn't hit me instead."

"I was aiming at you," Lewis said.

"Men," Susannah said as she drew Jackson to her and placed a rag over his bleeding mouth. "How can you joke at a time like this?"

"I'm sorry, Miss Moore," Lewis said. "Are you all right?"

"No," Susannah said. "But I will be, in time. So will you, Jackson."

"What about all of this?" Lewis asked, indicating the carnage around him. "I reckon we had better fetch the local sheriff—"

"No," Hickok said. "I'll be damned if I'm going to explain to strangers what happened here. We'll burn the bodies and not look back, and never speak of this to another soul."

"But—" Susannah said.

"It did not happen," Hickok said. "We are not here."

She looked around her and shivered.

"Yes," she said. "Thank you."

Thirty

"What will you do?" Susannah asked.

It was two weeks later, and Hickok stood in the street in front of Davis Tutt's saloon. It was early in the morning, and still cool. Susannah clutched a shawl around her.

"What I was sent here to do in the first place," Hickok said.

"You will be back?" she asked.

"When the war is over," Hickok said.

"How long will that be?"

"A few months," he said. "A few years. I don't know."

She nodded.

"I have something for you," she said, then placed her father's watch in Hickok's hand. He started to open it, but she stopped him.

"Not now," she said. "Look at it later. It is so you won't forget."

"I won't forget," Hickok said.

She kissed him slowly.

They were interrupted by Davis Tutt, who was leading a pair of saddled horses. He coughed and looked away, but Susannah refused to release Hickok yet.

"Do you love me?" she asked.

"Yes," Hickok said.

She smiled.

"Then I will wait for you," she said. "But you must promise one thing: When the war is over, the killing ends. You may have me or those guns in your sash, but not both."

Thirty-one

By the time Hickok uttered, "Thoreau," and was taken to John Kelso to deliver his intelligence, another six months had passed. Hickok reported on troop movements and fortifications, and the cave near Yellville where the Confederates were mining nitrates to make gunpowder. More months would pass, and the war in the West would continue, and Texan Ben McCulloch would be killed at the Battle of Pea Ridge, and the town of Yellville would be burned by federal troops. By the time the war ended, much of southwest Missouri and northwest Arkansas would become a barren district—but the city of Springfield would remain.

Thirty-two

July 21, 1865

Hickok was drunk.

He had been playing cards and drinking steadily for two days in the gambling room run by Davis Tutt on the top floor of the Lyon House in Springfied, and now—with the sun shining in through the window—he couldn't remember how much he'd won or how much he'd lost.

"Are you sure you want another hand?" Tutt asked.

Hickok tapped the table.

"All right," Tutt said. "It's your funeral."

Hickok poured another drink as Tutt dealt the cards. Then he took the watch from his pocket, opened it, and placed it open the table. It was just after nine o'clock.

"What is today?" Hickok asked, scooping up the cards.

"Friday," Tutt said.

Hickok was not happy with the hand. The best he had was a pair of nines. He took three cards and threw them, facedown, on the table.

"Do you intend to end this bender by Saturday?" Tutt asked, then dealt Hickok three more cards. "Or Sunday?"

"Look who is lecturing me on the evils of whiskey," Hickok said, then took another drink. "Next thing you know, you'll be asking my intentions about Susannah."

"And why not?" Tutt asked as he placed one card on the discard pile and took another from the deck. "If you aren't ready to declare your intentions, perhaps I am."

"That ship already sailed, my friend."

"Ships come back."

"And what is that supposed to mean?" Hickok asked, then threw five dollars into the pot.

Tutt saw the bet.

"Are you seeing Susannah behind my back?"

"No, Bill," Tutt said, exasperated. "You're my best friend and I would never do that. But you're about as hard on your friends as you are on your enemies. Don't look that way, Bill. We've been through too much together for me not to tell you the truth."

"Then lay on," Hickok said.

"The truth is that unless you quit drinking and stop these long hours and chasing after two-dollar whores, I think the best thing would be for me to take Susannah back to Arkansas."

Tutt placed his cards on the table. Full house.

Hickok tossed his cards, facedown, on the table.

"You've discussed this with her?" Hickok asked.

"Yes," Tutt said as he collected the money.

Hickok stretched.

"You both can do what you want," Hickok said tiredly. "I'm not stopping you."

"It's not what I want," Tutt said. "But things haven't been the same since the war ended. When we were riding together, it didn't seem like there was anything or anybody that we couldn't whip. Now, it's all gone to hell."

"I'm bored," Hickok said.

"When you're not bored, things are a mite anxious for the rest of us," Tutt said. "You came into our lives, and we welcomed you, and it was fun, but it was also like opening the door to God's own cataclysm—and it wasn't over until Yellville had been burned to the ground. And you know the other things, the things that we promised never to talk about."

"It was a dream," Hickok said.

"A nightmare is more like it," Tutt said. "Look, things are peaceful now. Why can't you enjoy it? You have time to play cards, you have a woman who loves you, and you have a best friend. You're lucky."

"Am I?" Hickok asked. "Am I up or down?"

"You're down, Bill," Tutt said. "You owe me forty dollars on the money I advanced you on this game alone."

"I have forty dollars," Hickok said. He pulled a wad of greenbacks from his pocket and threw them on the table. "We're square."

"And you owe me thirty-five dollars from last week."

Hickok stared at him.

"Thirty-five?"

Tutt pulled a notebook from his pocket and flipped through the pages. "Yes, it's right here. Don't you remember?"

"Hell," Hickok said, and poured the last drink of whiskey from the bottle into the glass. "Dave, I think you're trying to cheat me."

"You can't be serious."

Hickok shrugged.

"I don't remember owing you any thirty-five dollars," Hickok said. "Twenty-five, maybe."

"Dammit, Bill, you were too drunk to remember," he said. "I'm going to overlook that remark about me cheating you, because you're not going to remember that come Sunday, either."

Richard Owen, the new quartermaster at the Springfield post, had been watching the exchange from his seat near the wall. He had been playing poker with the pair until six, when he declared he had lost enough to Tutt.

"Ease off, Bill," Owen said. "It's been a square game."

"Well, now we hear from Captain Honesty," Hickok said. "Tell me, do you think I'm drunk as well?"

"I know you're drunk," Owen said. "Right now you're the worst kind—a drunk who doesn't think he is and who refuses to pass out or sleep it off. You're spoiling for a fight over something, Bill, but you'd best let it go until you sober up."

Hickok ran a hand through his long hair.

"Looks like I'd better go," he said.

Hickok stood, straightened his clothes, then reached for the watch on the table. But his aim was bad and his fingers brushed the watch, knocking it to the floor.

"Dammit, Bill," Tutt said as he picked up the watch from the floor. "You're going to break this in your condition. I'm going to keep it until you sober up. Why don't you give me your guns as well?"

"Like hell I will," Hickok said, suddenly flushed with anger. "I'm keeping my guns, and I'll allow that I will have my watch as well. It is my watch, Dave; she gave it to me and not to you. How dare you claim it over a thirty-five-dollar debt which I do not owe?"

"You owe me the money," Tutt said. "I'm keeping the watch."

"I don't want to make a row in this house," Hickok said. "It's a decent house, and I don't want Captain Honesty here injured during what might happen. But you'd better put that watch back on the table."

Tutt grinned.

"Are you threatening me, Bill?"

"You heard me."

"Take off those Navies and we'll see who threatens who," Tutt said quietly.

"Gentlemen," Owen said. "There's no need for this. It's a trifling amount. When the liquor and the anger pass, I'm certain your friendship—and your honor—can be repaired."

"To hell with that," Hickok said.

"Is it that easy for you?" Tutt asked. "Can you throw it all away just like that? What the hell goes on in your head, Bill? What makes you this way?"

Hickok was silent.

Tutt stood.

"Come on, boys," Owen urged. "Shake hands and shake it off."

Neither moved.

"Always black or white, ain't you?" Tutt asked.

"Don't wear that watch on the street," Hickok said.

Tutt left the room.

* * *

That evening Hickok left the Lyon House—where he had continued to drink—and made his way down South Street toward the public square, finally on his way home. His mind whirled as he pondered whether he could have been wrong about the debt, but the thought of Tutt treating him as an inferior made him even more inflamed.

When he reached the square, he passed a group of men loitering in front of the United Cigar Store.

"Is Dave Tutt on the street?"

"He's on the other side of the square, between the livery and the courthouse," one said.

Hickok looked, but his vision was obscured by a lumber wagon. He walked several paces to the northeast, then spotted Tutt, who was standing in front of the courthouse on the opposite corner of the square, some seventy-five yards away. Tutt was wearing a linen duster. His mind seemed to be on some other business.

Hickok drew one of his Navies.

"Look out!" one of the men shouted to Tutt.

Tutt saw Hickok.

He pulled the duster back and drew his Remington.

Hickok's mind cleared instantly as he rested his right hand on his left forearm and took deliberate aim. Tutt had taken an offhand stance and was bringing the Remington down just as deliberately, and the two fired at the same instant.

Hickok's view was obscured momentarily by

the cloud of white smoke from the muzzle of his Colt, and when it drifted away on the evening wind, he saw Tutt staggering backward, clutching his side.

He looked in disbelief at Hickok as he dropped the Remington and stumbled back beneath the columns of the brick courthouse, then fell.

Hickok wheeled, training the revolver on the men in front of the cigar store. "Is there any more trouble here?" he demanded.

The men backed away.

Hickok walked across the dusty square and, revolver in hand, knelt beside Davis Tutt. The ball had entered his side and passed through his heart, and he was now quite dead.

Hickok returned the gun to his sash and took the watch from Tutt's pocket.

He opened the watch and marked the time: six p.m. Then his eyes fell on the inscription: *Mark well the hours until we meet again, my dashing Bill, for life is short and death favors all—Susannah.*

Then she appeared beneath the shade of the columns, staring in horror as Hickok knelt over the body of Davis Tutt, the watch in his hand. She must have been nearby—helping Tutt with some business at the livery, perhaps—and she wore a pale blue dress, and a scarf of the same color covered her blond hair.

"He's dead," Hickok said.

Hickok rose and took a few steps toward her,

but Susannah backed away. She left the shadows of the courthouse, and in the evening light Hickok watched as she turned and walked across the square.

She never looked back.

INTO THE WEST
BY MAX MCCOY

A sweeping historical epic of manifest destiny, *Into the West* tells the story of the expansion of the American Frontier as seen through the eyes of two families—one white, one Lakota—over the course of many generations.

From the birth of the fur trade to the Texans' last stand at the Alamo, through the Civil War and the massacre at Wounded Knee, this is the classic novel of the birth of the West.

0-451-41188-9

Available wherever books are sold or at penguin.com

SIGNET

Charles G. West

**"RARELY HAS AN AUTHOR PAINTED THE
GREAT AMERICAN WEST IN STROKES SO
BOLD, VIVID AND TRUE."
—RALPH COMPTON**

OUTLAW

0-451-21868-X

SOME MEN CHOSE TO LIVE
OUTSIDE THE LAW.

Matt Slaughter and his older brother joined the
Confederacy only when war came to the
Shenandoah Valley. But with the cause lost, they
desert for home—only to find that swindlers have
taken their farm. When his brother accidentally kills
a Union officer, Matt takes the blame. Facing a
sham trial and a noose, he escapes to the West,
living as an outlaw who neither kills for pleasure nor
steals for profit. But there are other men who are
cold-blooded and have no such scruples...

Available wherever books are sold or at
penguin.com